TRACE CONGER

THE WICKED SIDE

A CONNOR HARDING NOVEL

The Wicked Side

Copyright © 2023 by Trace Conger

This is a work of fiction. Names, characters, places, brands, media, and incidents are either the product of the author's imagination or are used fictitiously. The author acknowledges the trademarked status and trademark owners of various products, brands, bands, and/or restaurants referenced in this work of fiction, which have been used without permission. The publication/use of these trademarks is not authorized, associated with, or sponsored by the trademark owners.

Cover design by 100Covers.

Interior design and formatting by the handsome devils at

Black Mill Books

ISBN-13: 978-1-957336-10-7

Printed in the United States of America

Library of Congress Cataloging-in-Publication Data

Conger, Trace

The Wicked Side (A Connor Harding Novel) — 1st edition

ACCLAIM FOR THE WORK OF TRACE CONGER

"Trace Conger is establishing himself as one of the most original voices in crime fiction." - Gregory Petersen, author of *Open Mike* and *The Dream Thief*

"Mirage Man is a propulsive novel that churns with energy and tension." - Vick Mickunas, NPR's Book Nook

"Conger's writing is direct. It moves clearly and quickly, perfect for thrillers." - Ronald Tierney, author of the Deets Shanahan Mysteries

"The Mr. Finn series breathes new life into the P.I. genre… It is one of the best detective series I've ever read." - Gumshoes, Gats and Gams

"*The Prison Guard's Son* is a superbly crafted crime novel. The characters are richly drawn with a rare combination of nuance and depth... This is one of the year's best books." - Mysterious Reviews

"*The Shadow Broker* tips a handsome hat in the direction of old-fashioned pulp fiction and it does so with considerable style. The writing is fluid and the plot pumps along." - Murder, Mayhem & More

For Jeff Hillard.

Thank you for your continued support and friendship. I'm glad I'm not the only one on this wild ride.

1

THE EIGHT HUNDRED DOLLAR GIRL

"I WANT THAT ONE." Connor Harding pointed to the young woman in a black leather dress. It looked like it had been painted on. She stood in a line of ten women, all trying to look more seductive than the others and all trying to appear as though they wanted to be there.

"She's more than the others," said the man in the dark suit.

"How's that?"

"She's younger. Younger costs more."

"How young?" asked Connor.

"You don't want to ask that question."

Connor already knew the answer. The girl was sixteen and her name was Anna Barnes. She'd skipped out on her hometown a year ago after an abusive stepfather took things too far. Her mother kicked the deadbeat out of the house and went looking for Anna.

"How much?" said Connor.

"Eight hundred for the hour. And you can do whatever you want with her."

The man motioned to Anna, who stepped forward. The other women retreated to a back room with looks of equal parts happiness and disappointment.

Connor reached into his pocket.

"No, no. You pay at the window."

"Sorry," said Connor. "First time."

Anna followed Connor to the window. It had a small cutout to pass money through. The woman behind it would have looked like a bank teller had it not been for the revolver on her desk. She smiled as Connor slid eight crisp one-hundred-dollar bills through the slot.

"Enjoy your time," she said with a wink.

Anna led Connor down a red hallway lined with doors on each side. All the doors were numbered, but only two were open. Connor followed her into lucky number seven and closed the door behind them.

The room resembled a posh hotel suite. The king-sized bed was covered in pillows. The kind hotels buy in bulk, the kind Connor found too thick to sleep on. Above the brass headboard were two paintings that could have been poached from a museum. On the opposite wall, a camera mounted near the ceiling pointed at the bed.

"What's that for?" asked Connor. "I wasn't expecting an audience."

"It's not on," said Anna. "It's for the cam shows. There's a red indicator light that tells you when it's on."

"You do cam shows too?"

"A few hours a day. Not with other people, solo shows. You can log into a website and watch me." She sat on the bed, removed her black high heels and pointed to a door under the camera. "You can freshen up in there if you want."

"That won't be necessary," said Connor, eyeballing the camera. "I'm not here for what you think, Anna."

"How do you know my name?"

"There's a man parked outside. Mr. Fish. Your mother hired him ten months ago to find you after you never came home. I'm here to take you back to Connecticut."

"What? How did he find me?"

"You'll have to ask him. I'm just the extraction team on this one."

"I'm not going anywhere," said Anna.

"Why? This what you really want to do?"

"No, I don't *want* to do it, but walking away isn't that simple."

"Seems pretty easy to me. We just walk out the front door."

"They'll never let you. They'll never let me."

"How'd you end up here?"

Anna looked away.

"Let me guess. Someone reached out to you online, pitched you some ideas about modeling or maybe acting. Promised to put you in touch with some high-powered people who could land you a job, get you a bunch of money, make your dreams come true. That type of thing. Got you to leave Mommy and come to the city to look him up. Told you all the great stuff he was going to do for you. But first, you had to do some work on the side, maybe pay for the head-shots. But then a few cam shows turned into something else, and now you're seeing men live and in person. You're in too deep and you can't leave, because whoever is running this thing is either threatening you or pumping you with drugs to keep you compliant. Any of that sound familiar?"

"I've never done any drugs."

"Then you're lucky. I suspect some of these other girls aren't."

"They said if I worked here for a while, they'd send me to California and get me a place to live. Sign me with an agent. Get me a modeling contract."

"There's no contract at the end of this, Anna."

"How do you know?"

"Because it happens all the time. They use girls like you until they can't get anything else out of you, then they cut you loose. Or worse."

"I can't go back to Connecticut. My stepdad—"

"Isn't going to bother you or your mother anymore," said Connor.

"How do you know that?"

"Because before Mr. Fish and I came here we went to see Rick. We made him a deal. He disappears from your lives forever and he gets to keep breathing."

"You don't know my stepdad. Threats won't stop him. He'll come back."

"Then Mr. Fish and I will go see him again. And take the rest of his fingers."

Anna slid back on the bed and pulled her knees to her chest.

"I can promise you two things, Anna. One, you'll never see your stepfather again. And two, if you come with me now, I'll get you home safely."

"They aren't going to let me leave."

"They won't be able to stop us."

"You don't know these people."

"I know the type."

"No. There's only one way out, through the front door. There's a guard. They'll stop us."

"They can try." Connor held out his hand. "Let's get you home."

She hesitated. "You don't even have a gun. They do."

"Didn't bring one. I knew they'd search me at the door. But don't worry about that."

She shook her head and pulled tighter on her knees.

"Anna, listen to me. If you stay here, it's not going to end well. You don't know what these places are like. You've got your entire life ahead of you. Don't throw it away because you're scared to leave. That's what they're counting on."

"They said they'd hurt me. And my family."

"They're telling you what you need to hear to stay. That's all. Come with me and this is all over. The cam shows, the johns, all of it. It's over."

Connor reached out his hand again. Anna rubbed her eyes and nodded. She slid off the bed and reached for her shoes.

"Leave 'em. You'll be faster without them."

Connor led Anna through the door back into the hallway. When he arrived at the window, the woman who had taken his crisp bills earlier looked up, confused.

Connor placed a hand on his throat as if he was chocking and frantically motioned her to the window with his other hand. When she leaned down and placed her ear next to the cutout, Connor reached through, seized her silk blouse and pulled her into the plexiglass.

"Give me the revolver and you get to walk out of here."

She began to yell, but Connor pulled her harder into the glass, muffling the sound.

"The revolver, or I'll crush you against the window."

She hesitated.

"Now!" He released the blouse, snatched the back of her neck, and pulled her head into the window. "Last chance."

She reached out with her free hand, found the weapon on the desk, and brought it toward the cutout. As it neared, Connor released her neck and stole the revolver from her hand.

Now free of his grip, she staggered away from the window as Connor pointed the weapon through the cutout.

"Give me the eight hundred back," he said.

The woman fumbled to get a drawer open and stuffed a handful of bills through the slot. He counted out $800 and tossed the rest on the desk.

Connor turned to Anna. "If you've got any friends here, you might want to tell them to get out now. It's going to get messy."

Connor stashed the bills in his pocket, checked the cylinder, and found the revolver fully loaded. As he moved into the lobby, a large man he'd never seen before burst through a side door carrying a carbine assault rifle. The man raised the weapon, but he wasn't fast enough. Connor squeezed off two rounds into the man's left shin and thigh, knocking him to the ground. When he hit the floor, he dropped the rifle and grabbed his leg.

A handful of women ran past Connor as he ejected the rifle's magazine and kicked the weapon down the hall. He left the lobby for the adjacent parlor. The women who had lined up for him earlier now cowered in the corner.

"The police will be here shortly," said Connor. "I suggest you get out."

They blew past him as he made his way to a side office. There, the man in the dark suit sat behind a desk.

"I'm not armed," he said, raising his hands.

"Maybe you should be."

Connor walked around the desk and blew a hole in his left knee. The man fell out of the desk chair and onto the red and gold carpet. Connor put a knee to his back and slipped his wallet from his pocket. Flipping it open, he found the man's driver's license as Anna came through the parlor door.

"Stephen Fields," said Connor. "Now I know who you are." He patted him on the back. "You see her?"

Fields writhed, face down on the carpet. Connor stood and drove his boot into his shoulder. "She's up here. You see her?"

Raising his head, Fields nodded, teeth clenched.

"Forget her face, her name, everything about her. Hear me?"

Fields nodded again.

Connor snapped the driver's license against Fields's cheek. "Come looking for her or her family and I'll find you. And I'll hurt you bad. Much worse than this."

Connor turned to Anna. "Anyone else here?"

"Just him, the guard and the madam," said Anna. "She locked herself in the back."

"Let's go."

As they walked back into the lobby, Connor found the big man inching toward the rifle at the end of the hall. He fired again, this time plugging the guy in the right calf.

"Stay down!"

Connor searched the man's pockets until he found his cell phone. He grabbed the guy by the hair, pulled his head away from the floor, and scanned his face to unlock the phone. As the home screen lit up, Connor released his grip clump and let his face fall back to the carpet.

He dialed 911 and told the operator that two men who ran a brothel had been shot and were bleeding on the floor.

"You're going to want to bring in the feds too," he said. "It's part of a sex ring." He left the phone on and placed it on top of a walnut table in the hall.

When Connor and Anna stepped into the sunlit street, Mr. Fish was waiting for them in a white minivan.

"Get in."

"Where are we going?" asked Anna.

"Home," said Connor.

2

———

NO REST FOR THE WICKED

Mr. Fish dropped Connor off at his Boston home. After several days on the road, the only thing Connor wanted to do was sleep. He thought about Anna reuniting with her mother. He didn't have children of his own, but he could still understand the anguish that comes with a missing loved one. The world is a dark and dangerous place, and sometimes you forget that when you're only used to the safe and shiny parts.

Connor went right for the refrigerator. The plan was simple. Enjoy a glass of root beer and then sleep for three days. He opened the bottle and poured it into a glass mug. He was waiting for the fizz to settle when he heard her voice.

"Where have you been?"

He turned around to find an old friend standing in the kitchen doorway. It was a visit he had been dreading. One he knew would come eventually, but not one he'd expected today.

"Hi, Zoe. Lose your phone?"

Zoe Armstrong stood with her arms crossed against a tan and cream cardigan sweater with a Native American print.

Her mirrored sunglasses reflected the overhead kitchen light. "Thought I'd get out of the city for a while. So, where were you?"

"I've been on the road."

"You still working with that washed up PI.?"

"We're all washed up in one way or another." Connor finished topping off his root beer, tossed the empty bottle into the garbage can, and walked past her into the living room, where he sat down. He knew an ask was coming, and he wanted to be sitting down when it arrived.

"I need you to go to Wyoming," she said, taking a seat across from him.

"I just got back home. I'm not too keen on heading out again."

"You need to think long and hard about how you're going to play this, Connor. You're into me for a lot of zeros and this will go a long way to paying that off."

Connor took a sip and the root beer danced on his tongue.

"What's in Wyoming?" he asked.

"Dirt, horses, and geysers. And soon, you."

Connor took another sip, waiting for her to elaborate.

"And my brother, Aiden," she said.

"I didn't know you had a brother."

"There's a lot of things you don't know about me. And I'd like to keep it that way."

Connor stared at his reflection in Zoe's sunglasses. He hated them, but they were as much a part of her as her long, straight black hair. It's who she was. But people's eyes tell you a lot about them. Their emotional state, what they are thinking, and if they are lying. But with her large aviator-style frames, he couldn't see a damn thing in Zoe. Just himself.

"What does your brother have to do with me?"

"Aiden is at the Hale Medical Center in Big Rock, Wyoming. They called me three days ago. He was in a bad car accident."

"Still don't see what this has to do with me."

She brushed back a strand of hair and readjusted her sunglasses. "I think someone ran him off the road. A hit and run."

"You talk to the police?"

"I talked to some guy named Hatson. He said they're not investigating it because they don't consider it a crime. They think Aiden fell asleep at the wheel. But that doesn't matter, because you're not going there for Aiden. You're going there for his daughter, Ellie. My niece."

"What about her?"

"She's missing. I've been trying to reach her since the hospital called, but I can't get ahold of her. I don't know where she is and that's a problem."

"Wife?"

"No wife. Aiden's been separated for more than a decade."

"How old is the girl?"

"Her name is Ellie, and she's seventeen."

"And you're sure she's not camped out at the hospital?"

"I'm sure. The hospital also confirmed she wasn't in the car with Aiden when it crashed. It's been three says, Connor. She disappeared."

"Maybe she's at a friend's house. Seems possible if her

father is in the hospital. Maybe she doesn't want to stay alone—"

"She would have called me. I'm the only other family she's got. Something's wrong."

Zoe's voice cracked, and for the first time, a trickle of emotion escaped her mirrored facade. She was rattled, and Zoe Armstrong didn't get rattled. He'd once seen her stab someone twenty times with a corkscrew to get a name and phone number without so much as a raised eyebrow.

"You think her disappearance is related to the accident?"

"I think it's related to Aiden. He works for the FBI. He's been in Wyoming for a few years, and I think it's connected to whatever he was working on."

"What does he do with the FBI?"

"I don't really know. He doesn't talk about it. It's a family courtesy given what I do for a living. Aiden and I are two sides of the same coin."

Connor didn't have to look far to see the irony. Zoe ran an underground information network in New York. She was one of the Big Apple's criminal elite and was likely responsible for more than a few disappearances of her own.

"Did you ask the police about Ellie?"

"Of course. They're as interested in her as they are about the accident. This is middle of nowhere Wyoming. Any local badge is going to be in way over his head on this, even if they *were* looking into it. I need this done right. I need my own man there. And that's you."

"Cops are usually pretty good people," said Connor. "I wouldn't get too suspicious."

"I'm always suspicious, and this whole thing stinks. I could smell it all the way from New York. Go find Ellie. If

I'm wrong and she's sitting at the library drinking iced tea, then this is the easiest thing I ever ask you to do."

Connor finished his root beer. "You're cashing in your Connor chip on this?"

She nodded. "Find her and we're square."

We're square. Connor hadn't expected to hear those words for a long time. He was into Zoe for a lot of money, the kind of money you can't repay, so he knew it would come down to favors. He just expected it to take a lot more than one.

"I'll see what I can find."

"I need you to leave yesterday. There's something going on here, and you're going to figure out what it is."

Zoe stood up and left without saying another word.

Connor set the empty glass in his kitchen sink and went upstairs to change his clothes. He didn't want to go to Wyoming. He wanted to go to bed. But more people have walked on the moon than said "no" to Zoe Armstrong, so Wyoming it was.

No rest for the wicked.

3

A NEW ARRIVAL

ELLIE TASTED BLOOD AND SWEAT. She couldn't see anything because something covered her head. It felt rough, like burlap. Blood trickled from her forehead and marched slowly down her cheek. Was her nose broken? She'd never had a broken nose before, never had any broken bones, but her nose hurt like hell and that seemed to be a logical explanation.

A man walked behind her. She didn't know where she was going, but whenever she slowed down, he pushed her forward. She knew it was a man because she'd heard him talking in the car. There were two of them then, but she only heard one person shuffling behind her now. Maybe the other one was too far behind to hear or maybe he stayed in the car.

"Where are you taking me?" she asked.

No answer, just another nudge forward. She was on a path, that much was certain. Tall grass brushed her leg when she strayed off the path. Her sandals kicked up dirt as she walked, and she could taste the dust through the burlap. It was draped over her head tight enough to stay on but loose enough that she could breathe without effort.

"Where are you taking me?" she demanded.

"Don't talk," said the man.

The last few hours were a fog. She had been in a car accident. She remembered that. Someone had pulled her from the vehicle. She was certain she saw him, but now she couldn't remember a single detail about him. Hair color, build, height, nothing. Was it the man who was behind her?

And where was her father?

"Stop."

She did as the man said, and a moment later, he placed his hands on her shoulders and turned her ninety degrees. She spun on her heels, convinced for a moment that she was going to fall, but he held her up.

"Steps," he said. "Down."

She eased her foot forward, feeling for a ledge. After a brief hesitation, she found it and inched forward, the man's hands still on her shoulders. Ten steps later, he commanded her stop again.

He jostled keys in his hand, and a moment later, a door creaked opened in front of her. Not like a rusty gate that hadn't been opened in a while. Rather, this was a heavy, slow moan. Like something from the bowels of a submarine or some sort of bunker.

The burlap itched her cheek. She tried to scratch it against her shoulder, but she couldn't get into the right position without crushing her nose, which hurt more by the second.

"Walk."

The blood found her lips again.

"I need a doctor," she said. "I'm hurt."

"You'll live."

It seemed like she'd walked a mile since reaching the bottom of the steps. Finally, they reached another stairwell. This time she counted six steps. Then another door. The man took longer getting this one open.

Was there a lock?

The door groaned when he opened it.

The rest happened fast. The man pulled off the burlap sack, kicked her onto the floor, and closed and locked the door.

She wiped her forehead and saw a streak of blood on her arm. When she raised her head, two girls about her age stared back.

"Are you okay?" asked the blonde.

Ellie nodded and looked around. The room was solid concrete. The floor, walls and ceiling all a stale, dank gray. No windows. A fluorescent light, the kind with two long tubes, projected a flood of white onto every surface. In one corner of the room was a toilet, and in another corner was a pile of light blue sleeping bags and bare pillows. Next to those were two pink duffle bags, unzipped, with various clothes pouring out. There was a single door in the room. It looked thick, like it could take a beating. Not a hollow-core cheapo one like at the hardware store.

"I'm Jen," said the blonde. "This is Regan."

"Ellie." She wiped her forehead again and picked strands of blue hair out of her mouth. "What is this place?"

Jen dashed to the corner of the room with the toilet and

returned with a roll of toilet paper. Ripping off a handful, she handed it to Ellie.

"I think it's some type of cistern," said Regan. "My grandfather had a room like this when I was a kid. Just a room for storing water. I think it's temporary."

"What do you mean?"

"There was another girl here when they brought me in. A few days later, someone came and took her away."

"How long have you been here?" asked Ellie.

"Maybe a week," said Regan. She looked at Jen, who nodded in agreement. "I don't really know."

Regan was a bit taller than Ellie. Her hair was deep red, almost purple, and it was cut to different lengths, but in an intentional way.

It was one of those styles out of a high-fashion lookbook, the kind that sit on glass tables at expensive hair salons. Regan wore a pink tank top with the creases still visible and jeans that straddled the line between dark blue and black. Two large hoop earrings the size of baseballs dangled from her ears. They seemed out of place.

Jen had long sandy-blond hair that was matted in some places and curly in others. She stood with her arms crossed in front of her plain white T-shirt. Her jeans looked identical to Regan's, as if they had come off the same department store rack.

"What happened to the other girl?" asked Ellie. "The one who was here when you got here."

"I guess her family paid her ransom or something and she went home."

Ellie thought for a moment. "There's no ransom."

"Of course there is," said Jen. "That's how these things

work. The kidnappers ask for money and then give you back when they get it."

"Did they take your picture or let you call your parents?" asked Ellie.

The girls looked at each other.

"No," said Regan.

"Then there's no ransom. If this was a kidnapping, your parents would want to know you were still alive. It's called proof of life."

"How do you know that?" asked Jen, handing her another clump of toilet paper.

"My dad works with the FBI. He talks about it nonstop."

"Then if this isn't a kidnapping, what is it?" asked Jen.

Ellie didn't want to answer. She blotted her forehead and tried to wipe around her nose without touching it.

"Did he do that to you?" asked Jen.

"No. I was in a car accident." Her head throbbed, as if there were something inside trying to get out.

"That's when he took you?"

"I guess. What about you?"

"I work at a coffee shop," said Regan. "This woman came in. She said I was beautiful and asked me if I was a model. I laughed at her, but she said she was serious. She gave me her phone number and everything. A few weeks went by and I called her. She said she'd need to take some photos of me to send to an agent or something. She set it all up. There was a photography studio and everything. I looked it up online. I went after work one day. She told me bring a bunch of outfits. She met me at the studio and took pictures for like an hour. Different poses and backgrounds. She gave me a bottle of water and there must have been something it in, because I fell asleep. When I woke up, I was in a van. They brought me here."

"Did your parents know about the studio?" asked Ellie. "Could they be looking for you?"

"I live alone. I was in foster care until I turned eighteen. Been living by myself for the past year."

Ellie gingerly wiped her nose again. "Did you live in Big Rock?"

"Where's Big Rock?"

"Big Rock, Wyoming."

Regan's face turned as white as the fluorescent bulbs above them. She closed her eyes, and when she opened them, they glistened.

"What is it?" asked Ellie.

"I live in Michigan," said Regan, burying her face in her hands. "I didn't know I was in Wyoming."

"Colorado for me," said Jen. "But no one said I was beautiful."

"What happened to you?"

She shook her head and wrapped her arms around Regan.

"It's okay." Ellie turned and tugged on the door. It didn't give. "It's going to be okay."

"How do you know that?" asked Regan through a faucet of tears.

"Because we're going to get out of here."

4

ON THE ROAD AGAIN

Connor arrived in Cody, Wyoming, the next day around 1:00 p.m. It was the closest airport to Big Rock that had car rental facilities. Given its small size, the airport was more crowded than Connor expected. When he saw all the colorful murals of Yellowstone National Park, he realized why. Wyoming didn't have a lot of airports—it didn't have a lot of anything—and Cody was home to the airport servicing Yellowstone. Most of the people rushing past him were on vacation, eager to see Old Faithful or those vibrant hot springs he'd seen in a Great National Parks documentary on PBS.

As he walked to baggage claim, he was ambushed by a kid in a cowboy hat who jumped out from behind a thick concrete pillar. The kid offered a "pew pew" and ran to catch up with his family. Connor hoped it wasn't a sign of things to come.

When he reached baggage claim, he found the same kid, but this time, Connor was ready. When the boy raised his imaginary Colt, Connor beat him to the draw, squeezing off two fast imaginary rounds. The kid grabbed his chest and fell to his knees in dramatic fashion. After a moment, he popped up, gave Connor a wave and disappeared into the crowd with his parents.

Connor always traveled light. He had a suitcase with a few essentials and a small padlocked plastic case. The suitcase was a quick pick up at baggage claim, but he had to go to the security office for the other one. His .45 wouldn't be circling the baggage carousel. Flying with a firearm isn't as tough as some people think. You just have to take the right precautions to avoid a long conversation with a pissed-off TSA agent or a Notice of Violation and a four-figure fine.

Carry a weapon long enough and you get used to it. It's similar to wearing a seat belt your entire life and then one day driving without one. You feel vulnerable, exposed. To Connor, a sidearm was as familiar as wearing socks. The military will do that to you.

After flashing his ID, the security agent handed over the black case. Connor stashed it inside his main suitcase and made his way to the car rental desk. Forty-five minutes later, he exited the parking garage in a silver pickup truck. He had reserved a sedan, but called a last-minute audible for the pickup. It was good practice to blend in on the road, and he was in Wyoming after all.

Big Rock was a two-hour drive from Cody. Connor had never been to Wyoming, and besides the PBS Yellowstone documentary, his only exposure to the state was his research on the plane. He'd read it was the least populated state in the country, which didn't surprise him. What did surprise him was that the entire state had about one hundred thousand fewer people than the city of Boston. That's a lot of empty space.

Leaving Cody, he took Highway 120 south to Big Rock. The highway was desolate even for the middle of the afternoon. In Boston, he couldn't walk twenty feet without bumping into someone the city was so congested with people. Here, he'd driven for the past thirty miles and not seen another vehicle. It was an odd feeling. Zoe said her brother had been in an auto accident, and while that was not suspicious at the time, given the isolation of this Wyoming highway, Connor suspected automotive accidents weren't common out here.

En route to Big Rock, Connor found it difficult to keep his eyes on the road. They kept wandering to the mountain range in the distance that had flanked him all the way from Cody. The jagged mountains jutted high into the bluest sky he'd ever seen. He'd always heard the term "Big Sky Country" but never realized what it referred to until now. A blue expanse, everywhere he looked.

The mountains were sharp and jagged, but every few miles, those gave way to sprawling plateaus that looked like they could house several city blocks on their tops. Years earlier, Connor spent several months in the mountains near the Tora Bora region of Afghanistan. These were more majestic, and less threatening.

The address Zoe had provided led him to a two-story log home. It wasn't the rustic log cabin one might imagine, rather a more modern take. It was an A-frame style with flat wood planks. Connor guessed it was cedar. The house had a large stone fireplace and a gray metal roof. It looked like a vacation home you'd rent out for extra income.

The home wasn't in a neighborhood, but it wasn't isolated either. Unlike Connor's neighborhood, where the homes were on top of one another, the homes here were a few hundred yards apart.

He peered through the front windows but didn't see anyone. He knocked on the door, not expecting an answer, but it seemed like the logical thing to do. If Ellie was home, it was going to make his job a hell of a lot easier. When his second attempt went unanswered, he made his way to the back of the house, where he climbed the steps to a deck that ran the length of the house. In the far corner of the deck, he found the grill Zoe had mentioned. Peeling off the black cover, Connor opened the cabinet to find the matchbox containing the house key. He slid the key into the deadbolt above the back door and unlocked it. Before he pushed it open, he peered through the windows looking for an alarm keypad. Zoe didn't mention an alarm and he didn't expect to find one. Given how far away the house was to any town, Connor imagined the police response time to a home alarm would be close to an hour. He also figured everyone around here had a shotgun readily available to handle any intruders themselves.

Satisfied he wouldn't trip an alarm, he pushed the door opened and called out.

"Ellie! Are you here? My name is Connor Harding. I'm a friend of your aunt Zoe. She asked me to check on you. Are you home?"

The house was quiet.

He moved throughout the first floor and called for Ellie again. Still no answer. As he moved through the living room, he passed an impressive coffee table made from a large slab of pine. Next to that were two chairs in the cowboy style, their thick red leather cushions emblazoned with a Native American thunderbird symbol.

Off the side of the living room, Connor found a home office. The walls were covered with framed photographs of who he assumed was Aiden and a variety of other important-looking people. They all had polished smiles, the kind learned from years of media training and focus groups. A planner sat open on the desk. Connor reviewed the entries for the month, but nothing seemed to be out of the ordinary. Aiden had no meetings scheduled the day of the accident. Next to the planner was a framed photo of Aiden and Ellie. They were at some sort of drive-through safari. A giraffe was pulling a carrot from Ellie's hand.

Next to the framed photo was a Polaroid of Ellie sitting on top of a brick wall. While he had no frame of reference, it looked like a recent photo. Ellie had striking blue hair down to her shoulders and wore a black T-shirt. She looked like a badass assassin from a video game. He snatched the photo and slipped it in his back pocket.

Moving up the stairs, he called out for Ellie again, not expecting an answer. He examined the two upstairs bedrooms and the bathroom but found nothing useful. When he returned downstairs, he slipped a sheet of paper from the printer in the office and wrote a note explaining who he was and asking Ellie to call him if she returned home. He wrote that Zoe was worried about her and that he was there to help. He placed it on the kitchen island before leaving the home the same way he'd entered.

The wind whipped through, carrying dust from somewhere. It dried Connor's eyes and forced him back to the pickup faster than he anticipated.

There were four initial stops on his itinerary. The first stop, here at Aiden's home, had produced nothing but dry eye. Connor hoped his second stop would yield more. He didn't know if Aiden would be awake yet but, even if he couldn't provide any answers himself, perhaps the medical staff could. After Aiden, Connor would go to the police, then investigate the accident scene. If he still didn't have any answers, then Zoe may be right, and Connor may be facing something bigger than he wanted.

5

THE HALE MEDICAL CENTER

Optimism had abandoned Connor years ago in a US Army Humvee somewhere between Afghanistan and Yemen. Since then, he looked at the world as different shades of shit. And while he hated thinking that everyone was out to get everyone else, he hadn't seen much to change his perspective. Connor didn't like that Ellie wasn't at home. She was a seventeen-year-old girl in the middle of nowhere Wyoming. If she wasn't at home, where was she? Zoe had been texting and leaving voicemail messages on Ellie's cell since she learned of her brother's accident. No return calls meant Ellie likely didn't have access to her phone. A bad sign.

The Hale Medical Center was twenty-plus miles away from Big Rock. Connor kicked the rented pickup into gear and tore out of Aiden's driveway, watching the dust kick up in the rearview mirror.

It was almost four in the afternoon when Connor arrived at the medical center. There wasn't much to the place. It was three floors of red and tan brick that reminded Connor of an elementary school. From the outside, the place didn't appear to be too advanced. What quality care could Aiden be receiving here?

The interior was more modern than the exterior, and whatever concerns Connor had in the parking lot faded away once inside. Whoever designed the medical center's lobby did a bang-up job. The murals of Yellowstone along the walls reminded him of the Cody Airport. Sculptures of Native Americans that looked carved out of rock stared down from pedestals. Each one depicted a different scene, and put together, they told the story of a buffalo hunt.

The lobby was the perfect blend of wild nature and modern comforts. Even the receptionist desk was made from slate. Connor approached it and ran his hands along the gritty tan and gray top. The woman on the other side of the desk looked up with the most authentic smile Connor had ever seen. Her plastic name tag identified her as Betty.

"How may I help you, young man?"

He wasn't that young but he wasn't about to correct her.

"I'm looking for Aiden Armstrong," he said.

"Aiden Armstrong," she repeated as she slowly pecked away on the keyboard.

As she typed, Connor glanced around the lobby to find a small coffee kiosk next to a waiting room that had a dozen chairs, all empty.

"Oh," she said, looking up from her screen.

Connor waited for her to say something.

"The car crash fella."

"That's right," said Connor.

"He's in ICU. I don't think they'll let you see him."

"Can I speak to his doctor then? I'm a representative of the family, from New York."

Her eyebrows raised. "New York?" She said it like it was some exotic land.

"Right. We haven't been able to learn much about his condition or how he ended up here. I'd like to learn more and report back to the family."

Betty pointed to the elevator next to the coffee kiosk. "Take the elevator to the third floor and turn left. There's an information desk there and they can help. I'm just a volunteer, but they can tell you more."

"Thank you."

When Connor arrived at the third-floor information desk, he exchanged a Betty for a Stephanie, who suggested he take a seat in the waiting area while she got an update from Aiden's doctor.

Five minutes later, a woman dressed in scrubs walked into the waiting area.

"Hello, mister…"

"Connor."

She shook his hand. "I'm Erin Duke, Aiden's attending nurse."

Erin had straight blond hair that reached her shoulders, parted in the middle of her head. She was nearly as tall as Connor and wore black scrubs, bright white sneakers, and several different-colored rubber wristbands. The kind you get for donating to a cause. She stood straight, almost too straight, like she had a steel rod in her back. She held a clip-board tight to her chest, and her defined forearms suggested she was big into fitness. Connor thought she might be one of those people who took training to the extreme. The kind who flip tractor tires, run muddy obstacle courses, and always talk about it.

"How is he?"

"Are you a relative?"

"I'm a family representative. His sister, Zoe, lives in New York. She's unable to make the trip, so she asked me to come in her stead."

"I spoke with Zoe the other day. We had a hell of a time tracking down his family."

"Shouldn't that be the police's job?"

She grimaced. "Usually."

"Look, I know I'm not a relative, but I'd appreciate any information you can give me. Zoe is really worried about him. She doesn't have much family left."

Erin nodded. "I'll be straight with you. Aiden's in rough shape. When he arrived, he had bleeding on his brain. They stopped that in surgery, and now we're just waiting to see how he responds."

"Has he been unconscious since the accident?"

"He was unconscious when he arrived. Since the surgery, he's been in and out. I talked to him for a few minutes when he was awake, and he knows he's in the hospital, but he's confused, which we expect. His vitals are improving though. I'd hope for him to be fully awake and aware in a few days. The fact that he's conscious at all is a good sign, all things considered."

"Did he say anything about his daughter, Ellie? Zoe's been trying to reach her but hasn't been able to. I went to their house and there's no sign of her. Could she have been in the car with her father? Maybe they brought her to another facility?"

"No," said Erin, still clutching the clipboard. "If she was in the car, they would have bought her here. We're the closest trauma unit in the area. Have you talked to the police?"

"They're my next stop."

Erin shook her head. "Hopefully they can help."

"You don't seem too keen on the local police."

She hesitated. "I just don't know if you can count on them, that's all. They're not used to doing much."

"I get that impression, considering it was you who reached out to Zoe and not them."

She shrugged. "I don't know if you'll get anything from them, but it's worth a shot."

"Given Aiden's condition, if Ellie was in the car, she'd be pretty banged up too?"

"Not necessarily. Aiden's injuries were limited to head trauma. While that's definitely serious, someone else in the car may have walked away without a scratch. Just depends on the physics of the accident."

"Can you keep me posted on Aiden's condition? It would mean a lot to Zoe."

"Sure." She took a sheet of paper from the clipboard and handed it to Connor. "Give me a number to reach you."

Connor jotted his number down and handed it back. "I'm not getting much cell service out here, but you can leave a message."

"You probably won't get that either. Cell coverage is pretty nonexistent out here. Where are you staying? Maybe I can call you there."

"Somewhere in Big Rock. Just got into town a few hours ago and haven't had a chance to think about it."

She thought for a moment. "Well, if you're staying in Big Rock, your only option is the Frontier Inn. There's nothing else around here. Just don't expect much."

"I'm sure that'll suffice. Please let me know if something comes up or if Aiden's condition changes."

"Do you want me to ask his doctor to contact you? He's not likely going to call anyone who isn't a family member, but I can ask if you want."

"Can he tell me anything more than what you've told me?"

"No."

"I didn't think so. Thank you for the information."

"I'm just glad Aiden has someone checking in on him. It's tough when we get people in here with no local relatives. It can be really lonely for them, as if they're forgotten."

"No need to worry about that. Aiden and Ellie are the only things I'm focused on." Connor thanked her again and made his way back to the elevator.

"Good luck with the police," said Erin.

"Thanks." Connor suspected he was going to need it.

6

GINNY AND THE FRONTIER INN

CONNOR DOWNLOADED DRIVING directions to the Frontier Inn before he left the medical center. Once he walked out of the lobby, he knew his Internet connection was going to dry up just like his eyeballs.

He retraced his route back to Big Rock and followed the monotone woman inside his cell phone to the Frontier Inn's parking lot. There were two vehicles in the lot besides his, each in different stages of decay. The Ford Taurus was the closest to death. While most of the car was a faded blue, the hood and one of the doors were red, and the trunk was lime green. The vehicle looked like a mad scientist had pieced it together using various car parts from a junkyard and then shocked it to life in a hilltop castle somewhere.

The Frontier Inn was the type of place that didn't care what anyone thought of it. It was the only hotel around, which meant it didn't have to compete with anything or impress anyone. The motel's exterior had been battered by years of neglect. Several of the windows were broken, a small part of the roof had collapsed, and the parking lot was riddled with potholes, one of which looked like it could swallow the Taurus whole. Connor counted twenty units, all facing the parking lot in a horseshoe pattern. The office was in the center.

He wondered if, like the Hale Medical Center, the outside of the Frontier Inn was a stark contrast to the inside. Connor opened the office door and stepped inside to see that wasn't the case. He approached the front desk to find a woman staring back at him. Her surprised stare suggested she wasn't expecting anyone.

"I need a room," said Connor.

"Here?" she said.

The woman's black hair was tied in a crooked bun on her head, and she smelled like incense. She wore an AC/DC concert shirt. It was from the Flick of the Switch World Tour, Cincinnati, November 11, 1983. From the looks of her, the shirt was twenty years older than she was.

"I hear you're the only game in town," said Connor.

"That's right."

"Why is that exactly?"

"Because no one comes to Big Rock. No reason to." She looked him up and down. "What are you doing here? Passing through?"

"Something like that."

"One night then?"

"Leave the tab open," said Connor. "I'm not sure how long I'll be here."

"Why would you want to be here any longer than you had to?"

Connor smiled and swallowed a laugh. "You from Big Rock?"

"Suppose so."

"You know anything about what goes on in this town?"

"Dude, nothing happens around here. Literally nothing. You could fall asleep on that bench out there for like an hour, and when you woke up, you'd have cobwebs on you. That's how exciting this town is."

He plunked his wallet onto the counter. "What's your name?"

"Ginny." She opened the motel ledger to a fresh page and handed Connor a pen. "What's yours?"

Connor opened his wallet and handed her a $100 bill. "How about we keep this anonymous?"

"Suits me." She snatched the bill as if it wasn't the first time she'd been paid to keep a guest off the books. After stuffing it in her jeans pocket, she turned toward the row of keys hanging behind her. "You got a favorite number?"

"Seven," said Connor.

"Sorry, that one's not available."

"You've got other guests?"

"No," said Ginny. "Toilet don't work. Won't be fixed until next week." She ran her fingers across the keys, plucking them like a string instrument. "My favorite number is five. How about that one?"

"Works for me."

She handed him the key.

"How much is a room anyway?"

"Twenty-two fifty a night."

"I'll give you a hundred a night, and if anyone asks, I'm not here."

"Why would anyone ask about you?"

"Nature of the business."

"What kind of business you in?" she asked.

"The getting-shit-done business."

"If you say so. If anyone asks about you, I'll tell them I never heard of you." She picked something off her T-shirt. "But, if I don't know your name, how am I going to know if someone is asking for you?"

"Connor."

"Alright, Connor No Name. Never saw or heard of you."

Connor turned and headed back to the door. "What time does the free continental breakfast start?"

"Eight."

"I was kidding," said Connor.

"So was I."

Ellie unrolled the blue sleeping bag. It was thick, insulated, something you'd take camping in the cold. She felt around the side and found the rough zipper. Running her finger down the track, the jagged teeth nipped at her fingers. She took a pillow from the corner of the room and tossed it on top of the sleeping bag.

"What time do you think it is?" asked Ellie.

"No idea," said Regan. "They keep the light on 24-7. Don't know if I'm coming or going."

Ellie looked at the overhead light. If she could twist one of the florescent bulbs out of alignment, she could turn off the light, but the ceiling was too high. With nothing to stand on besides Jen or Regan's shoulders, there wasn't much she could do.

She decided to stop thinking about solutions for a while, laid down, and closed her eyes. She stayed on her back, so her broken nose wouldn't touch anything. The pillow smelled of sweat, but she was too tired to care.

Connor spent the night outlining the investigation in his head. The next stop on his tour of Big Rock was the police station. He'd ask them about the accident, the investigation, and whether they had any information on Ellie's whereabouts. Zoe was convinced her brother's accident wasn't an accident at all. Connor wasn't there yet, and he knew whatever the local PD told him could tip the scales.

He had only been in Wyoming for a day, but it felt much longer. He didn't know if it was the flight, the heat, his irritated eyes, or the pressure of getting to the bottom of this case, but whatever it was, he was dead tired. When he looked at the clock it was 10:00 p.m. When he looked again, it was almost eight in the morning.

After changing out of the clothes he had slept in, Connor splashed cool water on his face, walked out of unit five, and headed to the office. Ginny was watching TV behind the counter. She had exchanged AC/DC for a Quiet Riot T-shirt. The one with the man in the straightjacket and iron mask. Connor's brother had the same image on a poster when they were kids.

"You the only one who works here?" asked Connor.

"Yeah. Hang on. I got something for you." She walked into a back room and returned with a Styrofoam cup and a donut. "It's that continental breakfast you wanted."

Connor took it with a thank you.

"You often buy breakfast for people you don't know?"

"Don't get too excited, Romeo. I'm just happy to see someone. It's been at least a week since someone stepped foot in here." She pointed to the breakfast. "And it's the good stuff. Well, the coffee is shit, but the donut is pretty good."

"I'll take this to go."

"Where you headed?"

"I was hoping you could help with that. I need to talk to the police. You know where I could find them?"

"Most people around here try to steer clear of the police."

"I'm not most people."

She nodded and sipped from her mug. "I guess not. Go out the lot and turn right. At the next road, take another right and then drive for about ten miles. It's next to the post office."

"Thanks."

"What do you want with the police anyway?"

"You hear anything about a car accident the other day? A nasty one."

"No. Unless it happened out front in the parking lot, I wouldn't know about it. Word travels slower than Christmas out here. You think the police can help?"

"I'd hope so. It's kind of their job, isn't it?"

"I'd say so, but don't get your hopes up, stranger. You look like you're from a big city. These aren't big-city cops. I'd lower your expectations if I were you."

"Funny, you're the second person to tell me that."

"Two and it ain't a fluke," she said.

Connor thanked her again for the breakfast, left the

office, and walked to his rental pickup. After climbing in, he devoured the donut and then took a sip of coffee. He hoped Ginny was wrong and that the police could provide him with something useful. She was right about one thing though. The coffee was shit.

7
___

JOHNNY LAW

THE BIG ROCK POLICE DEPARTMENT was right where Ginny said it was. Connor parked next to what looked like a brand-new F-450 pickup truck, the kind with the dual rear wheels and a trailer hitch the size of his head. It was decked out in enough chrome to blind anyone within a five-mile radius. Connor thought his rental truck was obnoxiously large, but compared to this behemoth, his looked like a clown car.

When he stepped inside the police department, three men stopped what they were doing and fixed their eyes on him. One looked to be in his early twenties, the other two pushing forty and sixty.

"Something we can do for you, son?" said the oldest of the three.

Connor stepped closer and eyeballed his uniform. The four silver stars on his collar identified him as the chief of police. His nameplate read Hatson.

The older of the two other men, a sergeant, was also named Hatson. Connor looked at the third, expecting this to be a family business, but his nameplate read Burton.

Connor took the seat in front of Sergeant Hatson's desk. He plucked a piece of peppermint candy from a crystal dish on the desk and popped it in his mouth.

"You recall a bad auto accident a few days ago?" he said. "One that sent Aiden Armstrong to the hospital?"

"Oh, that wreck out on Route 14?" said Chief Hatson. "A woman called me about that. Said her brother was in the car. You her husband?"

"Yes on the brother, no on the husband."

"What does it have to do with you?"

"Curious if it was an accident or a hit-and-run."

"I was on the scene," said Sergeant Hatson. "I watched them haul the wreck away. Called the tow myself. It was no hit-and-run. I checked the debris and the tire marks. Looked like a single-vehicle accident. No indication another vehicle was involved."

Sergeant Hatson had a blond buzzcut, a double chin, and squinty eyes that made him look guilty of something. His mustache was thin in the middle and bushy on the ends.

"I think that fella fell asleep, drifted off the road, and rolled his SUV," he said.

"Fell asleep?" asked Connor. "It was midafternoon."

"People fall asleep in the afternoon all the time. Maybe he was up late the night before. Maybe he'd been drinking. Could be any reason. Maybe he had a heart attack."

"I'm not so sure it was an accident," said Connor.

"Why? The driver tell you something different?"

"I'm sure he would if he could. He's currently unconscious in the hospital. Not too talkative."

"Uh-huh," said Sergeant Hatson. "Well, like I said, I

examined the wreck, and everything I saw was consistent with a single-car accident."

Connor turned to Officer Burton, who stood against the wall on the opposite side of the room. He was young, wore a wrinkled shirt that was a size too big, and seemed like he had something to say but didn't want to say it.

"What about you?" asked Connor. "Were you at the scene too?"

Burton shook his head without a word.

Connor turned back to Sergeant Hatson. "You mind giving me a copy of the report? Just so I've got all the details?"

Sergeant Hatson hesitated. "I never filed a report."

"Why not?"

"Not every fender bender gets reported," said Chief Hatson. He was a bit heavier than his son but had the same sandy blond hair, what was left of it, and similar mustache. "Lot of people around here handle those kinds of things themselves," he continued. "No need to involve law enforcement."

"Fender bender? Mr. Armstrong was taken from the scene by ambulance and is currently in ICU following surgery for bleeding on the brain. I don't think he will be handling this one himself, given his condition. That's why I'm here. To sort things out."

"And you are who, exactly?" asked Chief Hatson.

"Connor Harding. I'm a friend of the family."

"I'd really like to help you, Mr. Harding, and I sincerely hope your friend recovers quickly. But as the sergeant said, he's looked into the accident and doesn't believe it warrants further investigation."

Connor leaned forward and snatched another peppermint from the dish. "Well, then perhaps you can help me with something else."

He'd led with the accident to gauge how helpful the Big Rock Police Department would be, but what he really wanted was information on Ellie. They had failed miserable at the first, maybe they would do better with the second.

"And what's that?"

"Ellie Armstrong, Aiden's daughter. Seventeen years old. She's missing."

"Missing?" asked the chief. "From where?"

"From Big Rock. She's been missing for the past few days. Ever since that non hit and run. The family has been trying to get in touch with her but can't seem to find her."

"That doesn't mean she's missing," said Sergeant Hatson.

Connor bit down on the candy, splintering it between his teeth. "No, I'm pretty sure that's the exact definition of missing—not being able to find someone."

The chief turned to Sergeant Hatson. "Anyone report this Ellie girl missing?"

The sergeant shook his head.

"Why do you think she's missing?" asked the chief.

"I think it's reasonable to believe that she was in the car with her father."

"Then you should check the hospital."

"I did. She's not there."

"If she was in the car, she'd be in the hospital."

"You'd think," said Connor.

"Maybe she ran off," said Burton.

Connor turned and looked across the room. "So, you do speak. I was starting to think you were mute."

"You said this girl is seventeen, right?"

"I did."

Burton crossed his arms. "That's practically an adult. She probably left town."

"Wouldn't be the first time a seventeen-year-old up and split," added Sergeant Hatson.

"I don't think that's the case. I think there's something else going on here."

"And why's that, son?"

"I neglected to mention that Mr. Armstrong worked with the FBI."

"FBI?" said Burton.

Sergeant Hatson slid the candy dish further away from Connor. "What, an FBI agent can't be in an auto accident? You think there's something odd about that?"

"Is that what you're saying, son?" added Chief Hatson.

"What I'm saying is that if you look at everything together, there's something here. But you three don't seem to want to see it. You've got a federal agent in a town of what, a few hundred people? That agent is involved in an accident so severe it lands him in the ICU, almost kills him. And the same day, this agent's daughter goes missing. Hasn't been heard from since. Doesn't that seem a bit suspicious?"

"Look, you're entitled to your theories," said Chief Hatson. "And if you've got evidence of a crime, we'll look into it. But so far, we've got a vehicular accident my sergeant already concluded was a single-car accident, and I don't know a lick about this girl you think is missing. I'm not trying to be evasive here, son, there's just nothing for us to do on either of these matters. Now that might not be what you came to hear, but that's what I've got for you."

Police departments have a number of resources to track missing persons. They can file a warrant with her mobile phone carrier to pinpoint her phone's location. They can use the Technology to Recover Abducted Kids database to print flyers and communicate with the media. They could contact the FBI to ask for assistance. At the least, they could ask for Ellie's description and photo.

"You'd think you'd be a little more interested in finding a missing teenager in your town."

"Look, Mr. Harding, I'll be straight with you," said Chief Hatson. "We're not too concerned about seventeen year olds."

"You don't say."

"But that's because statistically they turn up. Unless she has a mental condition or is younger than fifteen or older than sixty. Those are the high-risk demographics. Everyone else, they usually turn up. Why don't you give it a few days, and if Mr. Armstrong wants us to look into it, we will. But we don't know anything about you, and frankly, a man coming in with no relation to this Ellie woman asking us to find her... Now *that's* suspicious."

Since he'd sat down, Connor had only heard excuses about why they couldn't help. He had hoped they would offer something that would lead him in the right direction, a nugget or a breadcrumb to put him on track to finding Ellie. Without anything helpful from the police, Connor would have to rely on the physical evidence to lead him.

"Aiden's vehicle," said Connor. "Where can I find it?"

"Benedict Towing," said Sergeant Hatson. "You're going to turn right out of the parking lot. About twenty or so miles out, you're going to come to an intersection. There's a ranch on your left. The Pale Mare Ranch. Turn left and stay on that road. Eventually, you'll come to a junkyard. That's where Mr. Armstrong's car is."

"It's unfortunate we couldn't help one another more," said Connor, standing up.

"Look, if we hear anything, we'll let you know."

"I'm sure you will."

Connor took a piece of paper from Sergeant Hatson's desk and wrote down his telephone number. He walked toward the front door. The corkboard that hung on the wall next to it was barren except for the seven red plastic push-pins waiting for something to do.

He took the Polaroid of Ellie out of his pocket, snapped a photo of it with his phone, and pinned the original up on the board next to the sheet of paper with his phone number.

"I'm not leaving Big Rock until I find Ellie," said Connor, walking out.

When he returned to his pickup, he reflected on what had just happened. The Big Rock Police Department clearly had no interest in investigating Aiden's accident, nor Ellie's whereabouts, but what he didn't know was why. Did they actually believe this was as simple as Aiden running off the road and flipping his SUV? As simple as a seventeen-year-old leaving town? Either they didn't know much about

Aiden's accident, which meant they were incompetent, or they knew more than they were letting on and didn't want Connor involved, which meant something else.

Maybe he'd get more answers from Aiden's vehicle.

8

───────

THREE TRAYS FOR THREE GIRLS

Three heavy knocks startled Ellie.

"Get back!" said the voice on the other side of the door.

The three girls stood up and moved to the back of the room.

The deadbolt turned and the door slowly opened. A man peeked his head into the room. "All the way back," he said.

Once the girls had their backs to the wall, he swung the door open wide and tossed a pink duffle toward Ellie's feet.

The man who brought the duffle was short and on the pudgy side. Ellie wasn't sure what she expected, but this wasn't it. Physically, he wasn't intimidating, but his voice was booming. He wore a one-piece coverall and Ellie wondered if he worked somewhere that required it.

"Change of clothes and a toothbrush," he said. "Bandages and medicine too. For your head."

He turned his back for a moment, disappeared into the hallway, and returned with three trays stacked on top of one another. They wobbled and he struggled to keep them from

47

falling. He carried the stack into the room and set them on the concrete floor.

"What time is it?" asked Ellie.

Without answering, the man shuffled out of the room and closed and locked the door.

The girls approached the trays to find three microwaved meals—it looked like chicken teriyaki over rice—three bags of corn chips, three peaches, three cans of Coke, and three plastic forks. Regan and Jen pounced on their trays. Ellie wondered when they ate last.

"The guy who brought the trays," said Ellie. "Was that the same man who brought me here?"

Regan opened a Coke. "Yes, but there are others."

"How many?"

"At least two."

Ellie unzipped the duffle bag and rummaged through it. Inside, she found a pack of three T-shirts and a pair of jeans that looked identical to the ones Regan and Jen had on. Deeper in the bag she found a toothbrush, a travel-sized tube of toothpaste, and a bottle of over-the-counter painkillers with three pills in it.

"You better eat," said Jen. "He only brings one meal a day."

"I'm not hungry. You guys take it." She looked around the room. "But toss me a Coke."

Regan tossed it to Ellie, who sat on the sleeping bag and watched the girls gorge on their meals.

Ellie gently laid the ice-cold can against her nose. "Does he come back for all this?"

"Yes," said Jen. "Maybe in an hour."

"You said there were others?"

"Including the guy who brought you here, there's at least two others."

"How do you know?"

"I've seen them, or at least heard them," said Regan. "One guy always brings the meals. There's another guy who takes us to the shower."

"The shower?"

"It's down the hall. I've been twice since I've been here. He's older, maybe forties. He likes to watch. He didn't touch me though."

"What's in the shower room?"

"Just a standup shower and a utility sink, one of those white plastic ones. It's halfway down the hallway."

"Are there other rooms out there? In the hallway?"

"There's two other doors, but I don't know where they go."

"Is that all you've seen? This room and the shower? Have they ever taken you upstairs?"

Both girls shook their heads.

"What about the third guy?" asked Ellie. "You said there were three."

"When they brought me here, I heard three different men talking," said Regan. "I've only ever seen two, though."

Ellie thought back to when she arrived. When she got out of the car, she had to walk maybe an eighth of a mile before she reached the first set of stairs. Why did she have to walk so far? Why didn't the car park next to the stairwell? Unless it parked at a home of some sort, and they got out and had to walk the rest of the way. The first set of stairs took her ten steps down and then another six in the second stairwell. Sixteen steps underground. Deeper than a standard cellar.

If she could get through this door, what awaited her on the other side? Were the other doors locked? She only recalled one set of keys when they brought her here. Could she unlock the others by hand? If she could get out of this room, did she have a clear shot out?

According to the Regan and Jen, they only fed the girls once a day. That meant the door didn't open often. Maybe once every two or three days for showers and once for food. Twice, for him to come back for the tray. If she could convince them she needed a shower, to clean off the blood on her head, she'd have a chance to see what else was down that hallway.

She removed the can from her face and opened it. She wanted to take the painkillers, but she didn't dare trust them. Who know if that's what they were or not?

After finishing the Coke, she examined the can and looked around the room again. She set the can aside and watched the other girls eat their meals.

What seemed like a few hours later, the door opened again. It was the same coverall-clad man who delivered the food earlier.

"Put everything back on the tray and move back."

The girls did as he said, and he moved into the room and picked up the tray. After looking through the garbage on the tray, he raised his head.

"Where's the other Coke can?"

"I've got it," said Ellie. "Can I keep it?"

"No."

"It's to take the painkillers. I need to wash it down and I didn't take them all."

He squinted at her. "Fine, but I'll be back for it later."

"And what about a shower? I've got blood in my hair."

"Later." He walked backward out the door and closed and locked it.

9

———

BENEDICT TOWING

CONNOR FOLLOWED Chief Hatson's directions wondering if they would lead him on a wild goose chase, or at least out of town. He was surprised when he arrived at Benedict Towing. Maybe the chief was on the level after all.

Benedict Towing was part impound yard, part body shop, and part junkyard. A rickety chain-link fence stretched across the front of the place, while a rotting, ten-foot wooden slat fence surrounded the rest of the complex.

Connor parked his rental at the office and peered through the fence. In front of him were acres of vehicles fading away in the sweltering Wyoming heat. The vehicles, which he assumed once wore vibrant colors and chrome, now all appeared a stagnant gray.

The office door was locked, but thirty seconds of uninterrupted pounding produced an older man who moved as fast as a tax refund. He wore a short, splotchy white beard and mechanic overalls, both spotted with inky stains of varying sizes.

"Whatcha need, son?"

"You Benedict?"

The man looked confused.

"Benedict." Connor pointed to the rusted sign peering down at them. "Benedict Towing?"

"Oh, that." He cleared his throat. "There's no Benedict. I took this place over in eighty-two. No Benedict then either. Don't know where that name came from. I'm Ned Turner."

"Well, Ned Turner, I'm here about a vehicle that came in a few days ago. A Chevy Tahoe that was in an accident on Route 14. Chief Hatson said I could find it here."

"Yeah, it's here. Whatcha want with it?"

"Just want to look it over. I'm a friend of the man who was in the car."

"I reckon so, but there's not much to look at." Ned opened the door wide and welcomed Connor into the office with a wave.

Ned walked Connor through the mechanic bay to a back door, which exited out to the main yard. Before following Connor outside, Ned grabbed a rag from the top of a swivel stool and stuffed it into his side pocket.

He escorted Connor around the side of the building, where the remains of Aiden's gray Tahoe sat waiting to be put out of its misery. Connor circled the vehicle, running his hand across the SUV's frame, careful not to cut himself on the jagged slivers of metal. He surveyed the damage and snapped photos on his phone from multiple angles. He felt like an insurance adjuster documenting a crash.

The passenger side window lay in large chunks inside the vehicle. The safety glass did its job and held most of the window together, but the force was still enough to smash it into three large pieces. White, deflated airbags hung from nearly every interior surface. Both taillights were shattered and the rear tire on the driver's side was bent inward. The top was bowed in, an obvious sign the vehicle had rolled after it was hit.

The driver's side of the vehicle took the most damage. That side was bowed inward, pushing the driver's seat into the console. The collapsed steering column dangled from what was left of the dashboard.

Given the condition of the Tahoe, the fact Aiden survived was a testament to American automotive manufacturing.

"It sure took a wallop." Ned squinted at the sun, slipped the rag from his pocket and wiped it across his forehead, streaking grease on his face. "It looks like something really big and strong hit this thing to cause that much damage."

"So another vehicle *did* hit it?"

"Shit, son. Don't take no college degree to see that. Look at it."

"Chief Hatson said the driver drove off the road and rolled it."

"Well, it rolled, but after something hit it."

"Would Hatson have a reason to lie about it?"

"Not sure if he's lying or just stupid. That fool don't know what he's talk'n bout. He'd just as much piss in your face and tell you it's raining." Ned bent over and ran his hand across the driver's door. "See this?"

Connor knelt next to the vehicle.

"It's paint transfer," said Ned. "You're looking for a black vehicle. A heavy one."

"If someone hit it, where's the other car?" said Connor. "You can't smash into someone, do this much damage, and then just drive off unscathed."

"That's a good question."

"And no other vehicles came in here? I suspect you're the only body shop in town."

"No and no. Nothing else came in my yard, but there is another place you can check. Owner's got a small shop next to his house. Does light body work, maintains the city vehicles and stuff."

"You see many auto accidents around here?"

"Just minor stuff. Some asshole talking on his phone rear-ends someone at a stoplight or something. That kinda thing. Not too many head-on collisions." He knocked on the roof. "And not too much of this type of thing. Looks like it was in a crash-up derby."

Connor returned to the passenger side and peered inside the vehicle. A brown cardboard pizza box was sprawled across the back seat and clumps of pizza littered the floor. He noticed the passenger door was slightly open.

"You open this?"

Ned shook his head. "I didn't touch the thing."

"Someone opened the passenger door after the accident."

"Could have been the medics, or the impact could have knocked it open."

Connor jerked on the door, pulled it all the way open, and crouched to look inside. Pushing the air bags back on top of the dashboard, he examined the overhead trim inside.

"Whatcha looking fer?"

"I want to know how many people were in this vehicle."

A moment later, he found his answer. As Connor ran his hand up the inside of the doorframe, he found two streaks of dried blood. It wasn't much, but it was unlikely from the driver. Any blood flying across the inside of the vehicle from the driver's side would have dispersed and would appear as droplets on this side. These stains were from a direct impact; the passenger's head striking the doorframe during the collision. He kept looking. Running his fingers up near the sun visor, he found two strands of blue hair.

Connor glanced at the passenger seat and ran his hand and along the thick seatbelt. The clasp was missing. He leaned in and felt around the passenger seat between the seat and the console until he found what he was looking for. The seatbelt's latch plate was still snapped into the buckle, but the strap was no longer connected. Someone cut the passenger out.

"You said there's another body shop? Whatever hit this is going to need body work too. Unless they just rolled it off a cliff."

"Reckon so, but there's only one other mechanic within a hundred miles. That I know of, anyway. I can't imagine he could fix the damage to whatever caused this though."

"You got a name?"

"Miller, Mailer, Milner? Christ, I don't remember. Something like that."

"Where can I find his place?"

10

NO ROOM AT THE INN

SERGEANT HATSON STEPPED inside the Frontier Inn and eyeballed the barren lobby. "Hi, Ginny."

Ginny looked up from her *Aquarium Hobbyist* magazine. "Well, well. Willie Hatson. To what do I owe the pleasure?"

"Just thought I'd swing by and shoot the shit."

"That right? Well, the sooner you start, the sooner you can get out."

Willie cracked a smile that neither of them believed. "You got any guests staying here?"

"Oh, sure. I'm all booked up. Turning them away, in fact. No room at the inn."

"Cut the shit, Ginny. I'm serious. You got anyone staying here or not?"

Ginny stood up, abandoning her magazine. "No, Willie. You're the only one who's walked through that door in weeks. I'm starting to think this town don't need a motel."

Hatson walked up to the counter and ran his hands across the top. "You sure about that?"

"I think I'd know if someone was staying here. It's kind

of my job." She pushed the ledger across the counter toward him. "Check for yourself."

He ran his index finger down the page and looked up at her before sliding the ledger back. "Suppose you're right."

"Why are you asking anyway?"

"I'm looking for someone. Name is Connor something. Just came into town." Hatson tilted his head to look at the row of keys behind Ginny. "Says he's looking for a missing girl."

"Looking for a missing girl? Isn't that your job?"

Hatson bit down and offered a smile. "I don't believe there is a missing girl. No one's filed a missing person's report. And this Connor fella, he isn't even from around here. Who knows what his intentions are."

"Well, I haven't seen anyone. And that includes your Connor guy or any missing girls."

Hatson offered another fake smile. "You sure about that, Ginny? You wouldn't be lying to me, would you?"

"Why would I do that?"

"Oh, I don't know. I mean this fella has to be staying somewhere. And you're the only game in town."

"Am I?" Ginny stood up straight, as if trying to appear taller than she was. "He could be staying anywhere. Maybe with someone in town."

"Maybe." Hatson scanned the lobby.

"What's this about a missing girl anyway?"

"There's no missing girl. That's all horseshit."

"Then why did this guy come to Big Rock looking for her?"

"He's got it in his head that someone kidnapped her or something. He's just confused, that's all. Maybe got a bad tip or something. That kind of stuff doesn't happen around here, you know that."

"Sure it does."

"Come again."

"That Indian girl disappeared last year. They never did find her."

"That's the reservation, not Big Rock. That kind of thing don't happen around here." He tapped his finger on the counter for emphasis.

"What does this guy look like? I'll keep an eye out."

"He's tough to miss. About six-one, maybe six-two. Solid guy. Short hair, short beard. Got some dark green military jacket on. Definitely not from around here." Willie looked into the parking lot. "Driving some silver pickup. You sure you haven't seen anyone like that?"

Ginny crossed her arms. "I think I'd remember."

"Right. Well, I'll let you get back to whatever it is you do here." Hatson slipped his thumbs into his duty belt and gave it a tug. "You be good now, okay, Ginny?"

He turned and headed for the door.

"Why are you looking for him?" asked Ginny.

"What?"

"You said you were looking for him, but you didn't say why."

"Because he's dangerous, Ginny. He's an outsider and he's up to no good. I can see it in his eyes. Poking around where he don't belong. Making up stories about mysterious hit-and-run accidents and missing people. Probably escaped from some looney bin. You just keep an eye out and give me a call when you see him."

"*If* I see him," countered Ginny.

"Right. You do the right thing and you call me. *If* he comes in."

"I wouldn't hold your breath, Willie."

Back in his pickup, Hatson clicked on his two-way radio. "Sergeant Hatson to Chief."

"What did you find out?" asked his father.

"Harding is staying at the Frontier Inn."

"You saw him there?"

"No, and Ginny says he hasn't come in. But he's here."

"I need more than a hunch, son."

"Ginny says the place is empty, but she's lying. The key to room five is missing."

11

MILNER BODY AND PAINT

CONNOR FOLLOWED Ned Turner's directions through town to County Road 50. He followed that until it ended in a sharp left turn. The pavement turned to dirt a quarter-mile later, and a half-mile after that, Connor arrived in front of a small but well-kept house. It was two stories, with an attached two-car garage. The sign staked in the yard read Milner's Body and Paint.

About a hundred yards behind the home was a building with six single-car garage bays. Four of the doors were open revealing vehicles inside. The last two garage doors were closed.

Two dogs, an old hound and a rottweiler the size of a wheelbarrow, stormed out of nowhere and stood their ground barking at Connor's truck. A moment later, a middle-aged man limped out of one the garage bays wiping something down the front of his overalls.

"Heel!" he yelled and slapped his leg. The dogs walked to his side sat next to him.

Connor stepped out of the truck and walked toward the

man, keeping an eye on the dogs. The hound looked like it was ready to retire to Florida, but the rottweiler seemed eager to prove itself.

"Sorry for all the barking," said the man.

"Just doing their jobs," said Connor.

"Yeah, they're real good at that. What can I do for ya?"

"You Milner?"

"That's right. Pete Milner. You looking for a mechanic?"

"No. I'm looking for a black vehicle with a lot of front-end damage."

"Huh?" Pete looked him up and down. "Can't right help you there, mister."

"A friend was involved in an accident the other day. Ended up in the hospital. Hit and run. I'm looking for the runner."

"Don't know anything about any accident." He motioned to the bays behind him. "All these are in for maintenance, not body work."

Connor stepped closer to the garage bays. The rottweiler stood on all fours but didn't stray from his owner. From where he stood, Connor could see a Mustang and three pickup trucks, in the service bays. None of the vehicles showed signs of a collision, at least not from the front.

"You hear anything about the accident?"

"Can't say I have. Then again, news travels pretty slow out this way."

Connor pointed to the closed garage doors. "What about those?"

"Like I said, I've got no body work."

Connor eyeballed Pete as he wiped his hands on his overalls again and slid them into his back pockets.

"This accident you're talking about, ain't that the police's job?"

"Guess they're not as interested as I am. They seem to think it's a one-car accident. I think it was a two-car collision."

"Why you think that?"

"Because I saw the busted-up Tahoe and the black paint transfer on the side. There was a second vehicle involved, whether the police believe it or not."

"Well, I don't know anything about it. Maybe check with Ned Turner. He's on the other side of town. Does some body work—"

"Already been there. He doesn't have what I'm looking for."

"Sorry."

Connor looked at the two closed garage doors. Each had four square windows running across them. He wanted to walk over and peer inside to quell his curiosity, but that rottweiler didn't hesitate a moment when Milner called him off. That meant he was a trained security dog. It also meant Connor was one verbal command away from fighting off a one-hundred-and-fifty-pound set of teeth.

Another time.

"Thanks for the information," said Connor, still staring at the closed garage doors.

Milner nodded but didn't respond.

Returning to the pickup, Connor fired the engine. He kicked it in reverse and turned the car toward the road, watching Milner's and Cujo's eyes on him the entire time.

12

ANCHORMAN AND LITTLE JOHN

"Your dad is cool with your blue hair?" asked Jen.

Ellie smiled. "Not at first, but he got used to it."

Jen ran her hand through her long blond hair. "I always wanted to color my hair, but my parents would never let me."

"What color?" asked Ellie.

"I don't know. Maybe one of those styles that's lighter at the tips and gets darker as it goes up. I saw that in a lot of magazines. I never really thought about it much because I knew it would never happen."

Ellie tugged at her hair. "The blue was a reward for straight As. Next year, I'm going to push for a nose ring, but that may too much even for him."

Regan hung her head. "Next year? You say that like we're getting out of here."

"We *are* getting out of here," said Ellie. "Soon. But I need to see what's on the other side of that door first. See what we're looking at once we get out of this room."

"How can you be so calm about this?" asked Regan.

"It's good to keep a calm head. It's the only way we're going to survive this."

"I mean, yeah, but *how* can you stay so calm?"

"My dad. He was a solider. While all the other girls were doing gymnastics or cheerleading, I was camping in the woods. We did all sorts of survival-type stuff. Nothing too hardcore. It's not like we were doomsday preppers or anything. Just basic stuff, like how to find and filter water, how to build a shelter, start a fire, that kind of thing. Life skills, he called them. He always said that in a crisis, staying calm meant staying alive."

"I guess I'd call this a crisis, alright," said Jen, flashing a rare smile.

"No, this is a colossal clusterfuck," said Ellie. "There's a big difference, but the rule still applies. Stay calm and figure out a plan."

"You're going to think of a plan?"

"Already got one. Well, part of one. I need to see what's on the other side of that door to figure out the rest."

Something metal slid on the other side of the door. It sounded heavy. It didn't slide all at once, but in small bursts. Pull, stop, pull, stop. It took effort. Ellie figured it was some sort of rusty metal rod, like a medieval deadbolt.

When the door finally opened, a man Ellie had never seen before stepped in. He was tall and took up most of the doorframe. Ellie noticed two anchor tattoos, one on each of his thick forearms.

"You." He pointed to Jen. "Shower time."

"I don't need—"

"I'm not asking."

Jen looked at Ellie and Regan, slowly stood up, and

walked to the door. He grabbed the back of her neck and held her steady. "You." He pointed to Ellie with his free hand. "New girl. You've got something for me."

"I do? What?"

"The can from yesterday. Cough it up."

Ellie exhaled, walked to the toilet, and took the Coke can from the top. She handed it to the man and sat back down next to Regan.

The big man walked Jen out of the room, his thick hand still on her neck. As soon as they were out, the door slammed shut. Ellie listened to the man struggle to re-lock the door. Pull, stop, pull, stop.

"We call him Anchorman," said Regan, "because of the tattoos. The guy who brings the food, that's Little John, because he's so small."

"Damn. I needed that."

"It's just a can."

"Cans are good for cutting. I was going to use it for something, just didn't know what yet."

"So what's your plan?"

"Not sure yet, but it starts with that door." Ellie moved to the door and ran her hand down the side. "Hinges are on the other side, and this thing is thick as an iron beam. There's not any way to open it from this side, which means we have to wait for someone else to open it. But that's twice a day with meals, more on the days they take us to the shower, but you said that seems to be random. They probably serve our meal at the same time every day, but with no watch, there's no way to know when that is. But this thing takes some time to open. Not much, but a few seconds. You heard him struggle to get it open?"

"Yeah."

"We'll hear him. We'll have some warning so we can get ready."

"Get ready for what?"

"To escape," said Ellie.

"What, just run past him?"

"No. If we run past him, he'll just chase us down. We're going to break his legs. And then we're going to run."

"Are you fucking serious?"

"Serious as a heart attack."

"How are we going to do that?"

Ellie pointed to the toilet. "With that. The top of the toilet. We can lift it off. It's porcelain. It's not too heavy to carry, but heavy enough to do some damage. We're going to use it to break Little John's knees."

"Just hit him with it?"

"Something like that. I'm still working on it. But that's part of it. You need to get used to the idea because you're the one who's gonna be swinging it."

"Why me? You look like you're stronger."

"Maybe, but I'm going to be holding him down. You're going to be hitting him. And you're going to have to do it over and over again until his knees buckle."

Regan shook her head. "Who are you?"

"My dad would say, 'Don't let the situation control you, take control of the situation.' That was kind of his motto. You have to make a choice, Regan. You can choose to wait this out or take control and do something. At least if we die trying to escape, we did it on our terms. We didn't just sit here and wait for them to decide what happens to us."

"How do you know anything is going to happen to us?"

"Open your eyes. We're not being kidnapped. We're being trafficked. This is the first stop. The next one, when they take us to wherever we're supposed to be, is not going to be good. It may not even be in this country. This is our best chance to get out of here. Our best chance to survive."

"How much time do you think we have?"

"Not sure, so we have to get as much info as we can as quickly as possible. I'm going to try and convince him to take me to the shower. I need to know what's on the other side of that door. See if maybe there's another way out or if we have to go out the way we came in."

Ellie crossed her arms and stood in the middle of the room waiting for Anchorman to return with Jen.

The girls were still waiting after what seemed like a long time.

"Something's not right," said Regan. "They usually only give us a few minutes to shower. Jen's been gone way too long."

"Do you think they took her somewhere else?"

"When they came for the last girl, before you got here, when they took her, they took her duffle bag too. That's how we knew she wasn't coming back. Like that goes with us to the next stop."

Ellie glanced at the corner to Jen's duffle bag sitting on top of her sleeping bag. "Hopefully she's back soon."

Both girls were pacing the room when the metal bar lock scraped against the other side of the door. Pull, stop, pull, stop. When the door opened, Anchorman appeared in the doorway.

"Hey, I need a shower too," said Ellie. "I've still got blood in my hair."

"Get back," he shouted, then shoved Jen into the room.

Regan caught her and they both fell to the cold cement. The door slammed shut as Ellie helped them up. Jen's hair was soaking wet.

It was also jet black.

Jen was breathing in spurts, almost hyperventilating as tears streamed down her face.

Ellie ran to the toilet and grabbed the toilet paper. She pounded her fist on the toilet top, checking its strength, then handed a wad of toilet paper to Jen.

Jen blotted her eyes, and Ellie wrapped her arms around her and pulled tight.

"It's okay. You're going to be okay."

Jen looked up. "My hair. Why did they dye my hair?"

Ellie's eyes widened as she turned to Regan. "The plan we talked about," she said. "We need to move fast."

13

BARKING UP THE RIGHT TREE

CONNOR WANTED to see what was inside those last two bays at Milner's place. The mechanic had no interest in letting him take a peek earlier, but now he wasn't going to have a say in the matter.

There was a gas station about ten miles from the property. Connor stopped and went inside. When he came out, he carried a white plastic bag in one hand and a stale cup of coffee in the other. He kicked the truck into gear and drove toward Milner's property. Clicking off the headlights, he navigated the rest of the drive by moonlight. There wasn't much out here, and Connor hadn't seen another car since he left the Frontier Inn's potholed parking lot. Headlights could cause suspicion, and Connor didn't want to advertise his arrival.

After passing Milner's property, he continued on for another mile and then pulled off the road, rolling across the dry prairie crushing sagebrush under his off-road tires. He stopped when he was far enough away that no one would see the pickup from the road, if anyone was even out there.

When he got out of the truck, he left the coffee but took what looked like a miniature fire extinguisher from inside the white bag and tucked it into his back pocket. Then he started walking.

This part of Wyoming was wide open and empty. Milner's property was isolated between two hills. The closest neighbor was about a mile up the road. Connor planned to approach the property from the back, hoping the dogs would be inside this late. If they weren't, he had a plan to deal with them.

Reaching the property's perimeter, Connor knelt on the dusty ground and surveyed the area. Milner didn't have any lights over the garage bays at the rear of his property, but there were several lights on inside his home. Since the garage wasn't illuminated, Milner would have no way to see Connor this far away from the house. So far, things looked easy.

Connor walked around the garage, keeping his eyes up for the two mutts. The unit looked the same as it had when he was here hours ago. The first two bays were still closed, while the other four were open, the same vehicles waiting for Milner's attention.

Connor moved to the first garage bay and peered through the square window. It was empty. He moved to the second and found that one empty too.

Damn. Where else could that vehicle be? It had to have sustained damage. Maybe they ditched it.

He shook his head and started back to his truck, defeated. He was nearly at the edge of Milner's property when he stopped and turned toward the house.

He remembered driving up past the house earlier in the

day. And he remembered the two-car attached garage. He assumed Milner wouldn't keep any vehicles he was working on in there. Those would be out back, unless there was a vehicle he didn't want anyone to see.

Approaching the garage door, Connor slipped his fingers underneath the rubber weather stripping at the bottom and lifted, but the door didn't budge. Had the door been locked from inside, he'd have been able to lift it on the track a quarter of an inch or so before catching the latch, but this went nowhere. That meant it wasn't locked; it was hooked up to an electric garage door opener. He could bypass it, but it was going to take a few items he didn't have but could find nearby.

Connor returned to the garage bays at the back of the property, slipped into one of the open units, and maneuvered around an SUV. He noted the logo on the SUV's door—three gold letters, PMR, with a gold lasso around them. Underneath that, the words Pale Mare Ranch.

He was careful stepping over the SUV's guts sitting in a pile on the floor. Behind the vehicle in a back corner stood a rusty storage locker. Swinging the door open, he found two pairs of clean overalls hanging inside. It wasn't the overalls he was interested in, it was the wire hangers holding them up. He slipped one of the coat hangers out, letting the overalls fall to the bottom of the locker. Then he searched for a toolbox.

It didn't take long to find one. Inside, he quietly pushed the various tools around, eventually finding a pair of needle-nose pliers. He clipped the coat hanger in two places until he was left with a stiff wire about a foot long. He used the same pliers to clamp the end and bend it into a U, fashioning a narrow hook.

He thought about the dogs as he replaced the pliers, being careful not to make any noise. Then he made his way to the house, crouching as he got close. The dogs must be inside because they would have already been on him by now if outside. He didn't hear any barking though, and he intended to keep it that way.

He passed the gray pickup truck with Milner's name on the side and finally reached the garage door. He peered across the lawn, giving one final look for any sign that Milner knew he was there, then he went to work.

Running his fingers across the top of the garage door, he found the center. Then he slipped the hook end of the coat hanger between the top of the garage door and the bottom of the garage doorframe and fished the hook back and forth until he found the emergency release rope. He wondered what color it was. Back home in Boston, his was red and white. At least it was until he cut it down to prevent someone else from doing what he was about to do. On the other side of the garage door, his coat hanger hook had snagged the plastic handle that was tied to the end of the short rope. The other end of that rope was attached to a release that disengaged the garage door from the drive belt that travelled across the track each time Milner pushed the button on his opener.

He pulled on the hook and heard a pop. The dogs heard it too, because a chorus of barking erupted from inside the house. Connor planned to wait for a few minutes to see if Milner would come out to investigate, but soon after the dogs started barking, they fell silent.

Connor slowly retracted the hook, bent it in half, and stashed it in his back pocket. He crouched again and slipped his fingers under the door. Lifting slowly, he raised the door up.

Inside the garage, a black F-450 heavy-duty pickup truck with a busted front end stared back at him. Its wide frame took up three-quarters of the garage. Connor stepped inside and ran his hand across the front end. Mangled pieces of chrome threatened his fingers. Both headlights were smashed, leaving holes where the bulbs once were. The collision was violent enough to buckle the pickup's hood, exposing part of the engine. Connor pulled his phone from his pocket and snapped photos of the damaged vehicle, just as he had done with Aiden's Tahoe. After clicking off the camera, he switched on the phone's flashlight and knelt for a closer look. It didn't take long to find what he was looking for. Paint transfer. Where the hood met the grille, he found fragments of gunmetal gray paint flecks. They didn't stand out against the pickup's black paint job, but they were there. It was the vehicle Connor was looking for, but who did it belong to?

He opened the passenger door halfway. Any further and it would hit the inside wall of the garage. Once he was inside, he clicked open the glove box. Behind a few napkins, a user manual, and a 9mm, he found it. The vehicle's registration.

The truck was registered to Tim Waters, who lived at 1053 Ashville Road in Big Rock. Connor snapped a photo of the registration with his phone. After stuffing the phone back into his pocket, he clicked the glove box closed and did the same with the passenger door. That's when it happened. If the dogs had been waiting for something else to spark their interest, that was it. The closing truck door wasn't much, but it was enough for them.

More barking exploded from inside the house. It was louder than before, loud enough to convince Connor that Milner had more than two dogs inside. He wasn't going to wait around to make a headcount. Slipping out of the garage, he yanked on the garage door and guided it down to the garage floor. He was a good twenty feet away when he looked over his shoulder to see the front porch light flare up and the front door open.

Connor heard the dogs behind him. He'd expected to see the Rottweiler from earlier and had planned to stop him with a well-placed boot heel to the head. No breed would shake that off, no matter how angry. He hadn't expected to see three Rottweilers. Yet, there they were charging forward. Connor lowered his body and reached behind him. The dogs closed so fast, he wasn't sure their feet ever hit the ground. Fifty feet out, he pulled the canister from his back pocket. At thirty feet, he raised the can. At twenty feet, he fired, blasting a putrid shower across the pack.

Bear spray. Effective on grizzlies and everything else.

The three dogs fell to the ground immediately, rolling around, coating themselves in dust and rubbing their heads against the dirt. Connor didn't mind hurting people, but he drew a line at animals. Like Connor, Milner's Rottweilers were simply doing a job. Connor respected that, but also had a job to do. One that would be considerably more difficult with a chunk of flesh missing. The effects of the bear spray would be temporary, and Cujo and his friends would be up and running again soon. Connor didn't plan to stick around to find out when. He retraced his path back to his rental, listening to the dogs yelping behind him.

He had nearly reached the truck when he looked back and saw a yellow beam of light sweeping haphazardly across Milner's property. Somewhere in the distance a shotgun blast, a warning shot, erupted into the air.

14

FULL STEAM AHEAD

ELLIE AWOKE to find Anchorman standing in the doorway. He stepped inside the concrete room, but only a few feet.

"You." He pointed at her. "Shower."

Ellie stood up and wiped the sleep from her eyes. Her nose still hurt, but the pain had subsided since she'd arrived.

Anchorman escorted her into the hallway and locked the door behind them. Her ears had been correct earlier. There *was* a metal bar. It was as thick as a shower curtain rod, and Anchorman struggled with it. He jockeyed it across the door until the end slid into a hole cut into the doorframe. The bar didn't look heavy, but the door must have warped over time, making it difficult to slide the rod through the supports. It reminded her of the fidgety latch on a particular bathroom stall door at school.

While Anchorman fought the lock, Ellie noticed something else. Someone had knocked part of the wall out to install the door. The room had been there first, and the door was added later. Regan was right. It must have been a cistern.

Once he conquered the lock, Anchorman turned and shoved Ellie forward, keeping her in front of him. This was the chance she was waiting for. She needed to see what was beyond the concrete room, and this may be the only chance she would get to find out. She'd note every detail and look for anything that could aid in their escape. Exit points, cameras, weaknesses, potential weapons, dead ends—anything that could be of value.

She walked slowly, taking in her surroundings. The hallway was dim, lit only by four single overhead bulbs about twenty feet apart. The walls were stone, packed tight, and had deteriorated badly. There were no windows, and she assumed they were in some sort of cellar.

"On the left," said Anchorman.

Ten feet ahead on the left was a doorless entry to a room. Across the hall from the opening was another room, but this one had a door with no visible lock. Ellie also saw a door at the end of the stone hallway, but it was too dim to see what kind of lock was on it, or even if it was locked.

That's the way out.

Part of her brain tried to convince her to go for Anchorman's eyes or stun him with a sharp jab to the throat and then make a run for the door. She could make it. It was right there at the end of the cellar. If the door wasn't locked, she could get out and go for help. If it was locked, she'd have to come back for Anchorman's keys.

Then the rational side of her brain kicked in. Anchorman was too big. Too strong. He'd stop her. And there were two girls in that room who needed her. They'd go together. After Little John brought their meals. It was safer in numbers, and the three of them could take Little John. That was the time to strike.

We'll only have one shot. Got to do it right.

"Here." Anchorman placed a meaty hand on Ellie's shoulder and pushed her into the open room on the left. "You've got ten minutes."

Inside the room was a square metal bin. The sides of the bin were three-inches or so high, and three-feet long. An open circular drain was cut in the center and a torn shower curtain with traces of mold around the bottom edges hung over it. Attached to the wall was a utility sink. Its plastic sides had decayed over time and were breaking off in chunks. There was a fist-sized hole in the front of it. Next to that was a small, white, plastic garbage can with a lone Coke can inside. The one she had kept earlier.

Anchorman stood in the doorway. "Go on."

Ellie stripped off her clothes, stepped inside the makeshift shower, and closed the curtain. She fumbled with the hot and cold faucets, which were tight to turn. Finally, she got the water flowing and let it wash over her. The sound of the pounding water drowned everything else out.

She welcomed the steam. The concrete room was cold and dank, and the steam coated her in a blanket of heat. She knew it wouldn't last, but she wanted to enjoy it for as long as she could. She found the bar of soap and went to work. While scrubbing her side, she doubled over in pain. She let the water wash off the soap residue and saw two softball-sized purple and green bruises near her right ribs. It was the first time she'd noticed them, as they hadn't caused her any pain until now. She clenched her teeth and waited for the stabbing pain to pass.

"Five minutes," said Anchorman. "Towel's on the floor."

Ellie continued scrubbing, being careful not to touch her side or nose. Then she washed her hair with a bottle of shampoo that sat next to the drain. After rinsing, she washed it again, convinced there was still blood caked in there.

"Alright, shut it down."

Ellie finished and turned off the water. She knelt on the hard metal and slipped a hand out from behind the curtain to find the towel, but Anchorman had placed it far enough away to ensure he'd get a show. She threw the curtain open, stepped out, snatched the towel, and dried off under the widening smile in the doorway.

"Let's go." Anchorman took a few steps down the hall toward the concrete room.

Ellie struggled to get her jeans over her still wet legs. As she hopped on one leg, she lost her balance and tumbled forward, catching herself on the doorframe. As she knelt to get her jeans leg over her ankle, she reached into the garbage can for the Coke can. She snatched it and stuffed it in her armpit, under her shirt.

"Move it," said the voice down the hall.

Anchorman waited for her to catch up and then shoved her forward. She stopped shy of the door and watched as he yanked the metal bar out of the hole in the doorframe. This time, she caught something she'd missed before. The only thing keeping the metal bar on the door were two C-shaped clamps. The bar passed through those and into the hole in the frame, but if the door was open, the bar could be pulled right out.

After opening the door, Anchorman pushed her into the room. "Back you go."

The door had already closed before Ellie noticed Regan's face. She was shaking, a hand covering her mouth as if stifling a scream.

Then Ellie realized she and Regan were the only ones in the room.

"Where's Jen?"

"They took her when you were in the shower."

"Where did they take her?"

Regan shook her head. "I don't know. I couldn't do anything to stop them." She fell to her knees. "I wanted to stop them, but I couldn't."

Ellie looked to the corner as the Coke can fell out from beneath her shirt.

Only two pink duffle bags.

15

A PLAN AND A WARNING

CONNOR FOUND Ginny caressing a cup of coffee in the lobby of the Frontier Inn. It looked like she had just met an old friend she hadn't seen in a while.

"Hey. You must have pissed off the wrong people," she said.

"That's likely."

"Willie Hatson was in here looking for you yesterday."

"The police sergeant?"

She nodded.

"What did you tell him?"

"I told him I hadn't seen you and that you weren't staying here, but I don't know if he bought it. There aren't too many options in town. I'd be careful."

"I'll do that."

"He also said something about a missing girl?"

"A friend was in an auto accident and his daughter is missing. I think she was in the car too. She's seventeen. I haven't had any luck tracking her down yet."

"Seventeen? That's prime age for running off with someone."

"Not this girl."

Ginny took a sip. "Do you think they know something about her? The police?"

"Not sure. But they aren't interested in helping me. I just don't know if they're inept, indifferent, or if they're hiding something. But I'll find out."

"Look, you need to be careful. The police aren't your friends around here. They can make things really hard for you."

"I suspect I'll cross that bridge sooner or later."

"I'm serious. Don't mess with them. Those Hatsons, they're trouble. Both of them. People talk, you know?"

"What do they talk about?"

"Just that they tend to do what they want. There's no one out here looking over their shoulder. No one keeping them in line. You've got to remember something. You're gone as soon as you find your friend's daughter, but the rest of us, we're stuck here after you leave. If you cause any shit while you're here, we're the ones who have to deal with the fallout."

"I'm not here to cause trouble. I just want to find the girl."

"I hope the Hatsons aren't involved."

"What about the third wheel? Officer…" Connor had to think of his name. "Burton."

"Kyle? He's okay."

"Kyle? You on a first-name basis?"

"Went out on a few dates a while back. Didn't work out, but he's not like the Hatsons. He's a Montana transplant."

"Dated, huh?"

"Despite its name, Big Rock is a very small town. There's maybe a dozen eligible bachelors in this place. I think I've dated them all at one point."

"Officer Burton didn't seem interested in helping me out either."

"He won't say anything in front of the Hatsons. Everyone around here is afraid of those two. Get him on his own and then talk to him."

"Maybe I'll do that. You ever date a Tim Waters?"

"No. Never heard of him. Why's he special?"

"Don't know, but I plan to find out." Connor headed for the door.

"Hey, I'm sorry about the girl you're looking for. I hope you find her."

"I'll find her." Connor thought for a moment. "If you were seventeen again, where would you go if you were looking for trouble?"

"Was she looking for trouble?"

"I don't know if she was looking for it, but she found it. Or it found her."

Ginny considered the question. "Probably the Hunting Lodge."

"What's that?"

"A bar. If you can call it that. Get a lot of ranch hands and cowboys out there. They used to run a prostitution ring out of the barn in the back. Kind of place where daddies brought their sons to get their first piece of ass, that sort of thing. Not sure if that's still happening."

"Classy."

"Rumor was that Chief Hatson knew about it but looked

the other way. I've been there a few times when I was younger and dumber. It's not a place I'd go back to. Drunk, aggressive men who don't take no for an answer aren't really my type."

"This place is still open?"

"It's open. A while ago, this Indian girl went missing from the Shoshone Reservation. Indian Affairs and the FBI came to town for a few days, and I know they were out there asking questions. I don't think anything ever came of it though. They were here too. Asked me if anyone had been staying here near the time she went missing. That was an easy one to answer."

"Did they ever find her?"

Ginny shook her head. "Don't think so."

"Do you remember the person you talked to?"

"No, but they left a card. I may still have it."

Ginny disappeared into a back office and returned a minute later flapping a business card across her palm. "Here you go." She handed it to Connor. "Kept it in the top desk drawer. Never seen an FBI business card before. Seemed like something to hang on to."

"Thanks." Connor stuffed the card in his wallet. "This Hunting Lodge. How do I find it?"

"You can't miss it. Turn left out of the parking lot and keep driving about an hour. You'll run into it eventually."

"Thanks." Connor headed for the door again.

"They won't be open this early though."

"Not going there now. I'm going to go see your boyfriend and his boss. See why they aren't interested in my missing girl."

"He's not my boyfriend."

. . .

Ellie took the Coke can, wrapped her fingers around it and pressed tightly, collapsing the middle. Then she bent the top and bottom back and forth until she weakened the aluminum enough to tear it into two pieces.

"What are you doing," asked Regan, standing over her.

Ellie grabbed her sleeping bag and found the zipper. "We're going to have to take out Little John when he comes back. I think this will help." She picked up half of the can and used its jagged edge to cut into the light blue material. Sawing through the sleeping bag, she carefully cut away the zipper and the black nylon strip it was attached to.

When she had cut through the final stitch attaching the zipper, she held it in front of her and pulled tight, testing the nylon's strength.

"We need to be ready the next time that door opens."

"What are we going to do?"

Ellie stood up and walked to the toilet, where she lifted the porcelain top from the tank, placed it on the floor in the center of the room, and draped a sleeping bag over it. She took her sleeping bag with the missing zipper and tossed it over the toilet to conceal the missing lid.

"The metal bar on the other side of the door sticks. We'll hear it move and we'll have a few seconds to get into place. As soon as that door opens, we attack. Once we start, we don't stop until it's over. We've got to commit."

"What do I do?"

"As soon as Little John comes through that doorway, I'm going for his throat. I can get this cord around his neck. He's going to struggle and try to fight me off, but I'm going to hang on as tight as I can. That's when you're going to pick up that lid and start swinging. Go for his knees so you don't hit me by mistake. Now, he's going to be kicking and thrashing, so he's going to be tough to hit, but you keep swinging. You keep hitting his legs until he stops moving or until that lid breaks into a thousand pieces, whichever comes first."

"On my God. Are we going to kill him?"

"It's him or us, Regan."

"How do we know he's going to be alone? What if there's two of them?"

"Little John is always alone."

"But what if there's someone else in the hall? Someone we couldn't see before? Someone else out there waiting?"

"When Little John brings the trays, he carries them all himself. He almost dropped one before. If there was someone with him, they'd probably be carrying a tray. He's alone."

"What if we get out? Then what? We don't know what's on the other side of that door."

"Sure we do," said Ellie. "At the end of that hallway is another door and—"

"What if that one is locked?"

"Little John will have a key. He'd have to unlock any door for himself. We go out the same way he would."

"What if he doesn't have a key? What if someone else let him in? Maybe they're on the other side of that door. As a precaution."

"Then we go through them. When I went to the shower, I looked around that hallway. Everything is old and decrepit. If the door is locked from the outside and Little John doesn't have a key, then we take that bar to it and knock the shit out of it until it falls over. Then we go to work on whoever is behind it."

Regan put her hands on her face and shook her head. "I don't know."

"Look, Regan, you don't know me, but I don't half-ass anything. If I didn't think we could get out of here, then I wouldn't try it. We can do this."

"Maybe you're right." She raised her head with new life in her eyes. "Yeah. Fuck yeah, we can."

Ellie had no idea when that door would open. She'd lost all sense of time. She didn't even know how long she'd been in the concrete room. She'd eaten four times, but didn't know how many meals they gave her each day. If it was one, she'd have been here for four days. On one hand, that seemed impossible, but on the other, it seemed right. She didn't know if she had eaten today or not.

She moved to the center of the room and sat down, gripping the cord tight in her hand. Regan sat down next to her and they focused on the door.

And waited.

When Connor arrived at the Big Rock Police Department, he found the place just as he'd left it a few days earlier. Chief Hatson was locked away in his back office, Sergeant Hatson was on the phone, no doubt trying to make Daddy proud, and no one seemed excited to see him. The only thing missing was Officer Burton.

Connor took a seat across from the sergeant and stared him down, waiting for him to finish his call, something about a missing RV. Visibly annoyed, the younger Hatson scribbled his final note on his pad and hung up the phone.

"Right in the middle of something," he said. "What you need?"

Connor removed a piece of paper from his pocket, set it on the sergeant's desk and hammered it with his fist.

"I'm here to report a hit-and-run."

Connor's broad hand meeting the top of Hatson's cheap particle-board desk must have attracted the chief's attention, because he stopped whatever he was doing in his office and stepped into the main room.

"What is this about a hit-and-run?" said Sergeant Hatson.

"You remember the last time I came in here barking about an auto accident and a missing girl, the girl you refused to investigate?"

No one took the bait.

"And remember how I said I was going to look into it?"

Silence still.

"The name on that paper, Tim Waters." Connor tapped it with his index finger. "He owns the F-450 that knocked Aiden Armstrong off the road and put him in the hospital. And I want you to go talk to him."

"And he has what to do with your missing girl?" asked the sergeant.

"Tim Waters lives here in Big Rock. And if he was driving that truck when it hit Aiden, then he was likely the last person to see Ellie before she went missing."

"How does a hit-and-run turn into a missing person?" said Sergeant Hatson. "I don't see the connection."

"Ellie Armstrong was in that car when it was run off the road. When the ambulance showed up, she was gone."

"How do you know she was in the car?"

"There's blood on the passenger doorframe."

"And you know this is her blood?"

"Yes."

"Hold on a minute," said Chief Hatson. "You're basing all this on some vehicle you found. How do you know this is the same vehicle that hit your friend?"

"Paint transfer. And the damage profile fits. I saw both vehicles." He tapped on the note again. "This is the one."

"And where did you find this vehicle?"

"That's privileged information."

"It wouldn't happen to be at Milner's Garage would it?" asked Chief Hatson.

Connor kept his mouth shut.

"Because he called me late last night yelling about someone sneaking onto his property and macing his dogs. Said he spent two hours washing their eyes out. Not an easy task given the breed."

The sergeant crossed his arms. "You know anything about that?"

"Not a thing," said Connor.

"I don't believe that."

"I don't care what you believe. The only thing I care about is you looking into this Tim Waters and seeing if he knows anything about Ellie. Then after you press him on that, you can arrest him on hit-and-run charges."

"You got a lot of nerve coming in here and telling me what to do in my own town, son."

"I'm giving you the chance to do the right thing, Chief. You can go over there and question him about Ellie Armstrong's whereabouts or I can."

Chief Hatson snatched the paper from his son's desk. "You'll do no such thing. You go talk to that man, or anyone else, and you'll end up right back here. In cuffs. If you came to Big Rock looking for vigilante justice, you're not going to find it. That's not how we do things around here."

"Seems you don't do anything around here. I've asked you to look into a missing person and you're dicking around like she's got all the time in the world. I've just given you a suspect, and instead of making the slightest effort to go talk to him, you're telling me all the reasons you can't. At least make a goddamn effort."

"Son, I told you before and I'll tell you again, you're barking up the wrong tree. You're trying to make a case out of nothing. Now if you continue to break into homes and cause trouble, we might have to escort you out of town."

Connor stood up. "You're welcome to try."

Most police departments would want to get to the bottom of this, even if it was simply to prove Connor wrong and send him on his way. Big Rock wasn't most police departments. It was obvious they were more concerned about circling the wagons than doing anything remotely resembling police work. They were hiding something, and Connor was more determined than ever to find out what. He was nearly out of the building when Chief Hatson barked back.

"You stay away from Tim Waters or I will lock you up!"

The words lingered behind Connor as he left the police department.

16

AN UNLIKELY ALLY

ACCORDING to the registration in the busted F-450's glove box, Tim Waters lived at 1053 Ashville Road. He was the first solid lead Connor had, and he planned to introduce himself to Tim the first chance he got.

The address was in a development called the Mountain View Community. Connor rolled through the open gate to find rows upon rows of manufactured homes. They were all painted beige and blended into the mountains behind them. The only thing differentiating one unit from the next was the address numbers on the front of each house. Everything else about the units was identical, from the wooden park benches in the backyards, to the rows of yellow and purple flowers flanking the parking pads, to the young trees staked in the front yards. Connor wondered if anyone ever walked into the wrong home by mistake. The similarities made that a real possibility.

Rolling through the community, Connor stopped in front of unit 1053. The parking pad next to the home was empty, but that didn't mean Tim wasn't home. After all, his pickup was inside Milner's garage. While Tim's pickup wasn't there, another vehicle of interest was. Parked on the side of the street six homes down from Tim's place was a police cruiser. It was a lookout, and it was looking for Connor. He was certain the Big Rock PD was ready to arrest him as soon as he did something to warrant it, and breaking and entering fit the bill.

Connor kicked the truck in gear, turned around in one of the vacant parking pads and drove in the other direction. He drove around the road surrounding the community and came to a stop a few car lengths behind the cruiser. He approached the side of the vehicle, keeping his empty hands in plain sight. When he tapped on the cruiser's passenger window, Office Burton rolled it down.

"Looking for me?" said Connor.

"You basically told us you were coming here," said Burton. "The chief radioed saying you threw a fit at the station. He told me to wait for you here. Said you were going to do something stupid."

"I hear you're one of the more level-headed people in Big Rock."

"I like to think so."

"I also know you're not big on talking around the Hatsons. They keep a tight leash on you?"

"No leash. Chain of command is all. I've only been here for six months. Moved from Montana."

"So, you're still eager to do the right thing? To help people?"

"Of course, but I'm also eager to protect the citizens of Big Rock from vigilantes."

"That's what you think I am?"

"They said you're here to threaten Tim Waters, and last I checked, that's illegal. Even in Wyoming."

"I can't ask questions about a missing girl?"

"You can ask all the questions you want, as long as you keep it civil. Lot of people around here don't take kindly to outsiders making threats and throwing their weight around. Might get yourself hurt."

"I can take care of myself."

"I bet."

Connor looked over the cruiser's red and blue light bar at Tim's home. "You got kids, Officer?"

"No."

"Then maybe you can't appreciate my predicament. I'm looking for a missing girl, and the longer she stays missing, the harder it's going to be to find her."

"I understand that."

"I don't think you do, because the Big Rock Police Department has done jack shit to help."

"Sergeant Hatson went to her home to check things out. He told me he's looking into it."

"I don't trust Sergeant Hatson to wipe my ass, let alone find a missing person. Besides, the sergeant seems to have no interest in following up on my Tim Waters lead. Why's that?"

"Tim and Sergeant Hatson are friends. I've seen him in the station before. They go to lunch together, that sort of thing. If he thinks Tim has nothing to do with this, then he likely doesn't."

Connor focused on the windows, trying to see any movement inside. "Really? I bring in clear evidence that Waters's truck was involved in the hit-and-run that put a man in ICU

—a man whose daughter was in that car and is now missing —and Waters gets a pass? Not even going to have the conversation, because he and one third of the local PD are friends? You realize how ridiculous that sounds?"

Burton didn't have an answer.

"How well do you know the Hatsons?"

"Well enough."

"What about the missing Indian girl?"

"What about her?" asked Burton.

"You ever find her?"

"That was before my time, but Indian girls go missing. It happens. Too frequently, I'll admit, but what does that have to do with your friend?"

"Look, I'm barreling toward a dead end here, and Tim Waters is the only lead I have. I need to talk to him."

Burton shook his head. "He's not home."

"Where is he?"

"He's a ranch hand. I suspect he's at the ranch."

"And which ranch is that?"

Burton shook his head again. "I have a bad feeling of what may happen if I put you and Mr. Waters together, and I sure as hell don't need you going to his place of business and causing trouble."

"What makes you think I'll cause trouble?"

"I can tell you're trouble just by looking at you. It's not my first rodeo. As I said, Montana transplant. Listen, I want to help you. I don't like the idea of a missing girl any more than you do, but I also swore an oath to protect the citizens of Big Rock and uphold the law. And that's what I intend to do. I'm sure we can figure out a way I can do both."

"Then why don't *you* go have a chat with Tim Waters?

Ask him why his pickup truck knocked Aiden Armstrong's SUV off the road and put him in the hospital. Then ask him why Ellie was in the car during the accident but never made it to the hospital. Seems he's the last person to come into contact with her."

"There's no evidence he came into contact with anyone."

"See, now you're thinking like a Hatson. You've shut your mind off to even the possibility Waters is involved. How does that support that oath you were yapping about?"

Burton thought for a moment. "Suppose you got a point there. Okay, I'll have a chat with Mr. Waters and see if he can shed any light on this."

"At the very least, he's involved in a hit-and-run, if not a child abduction."

"That's quite a leap," said Burton. "I'll talk to him and see what he has to say."

Connor searched his pocket for his notepad.

"I've already got your number," said Burton. "I wrote it down the first time you came in. Surprised?"

"Actually, I am."

"I'm a good cop. I'll help however I can, but I'm going to do it the right way."

Connor stepped away from the cruiser, as Officer Burton started the engine.

"And Harding? If I find out you went into that house, I'll haul you in. You understand?"

Connor didn't say anything as Officer Burton kicked the cruiser into gear and rolled toward the main road.

Connor didn't play nice with the police. He didn't have anything against the boys in blue, he just often found himself on the opposite side of the fence. Maybe Officer Burton could help after all. He seemed like a genuine human who had yet to part with his rose-colored glasses. Connor had lost his a long time ago.

While Burton began his investigation, Connor continued his. The back of Tim Waters's home butted up against a row of trees, and while it wasn't completely hidden, at this time of day Connor didn't think there would be a lot of eyeballs on it. He walked up the three pressure-treated wooden steps and knocked on the back door. No answer. Maybe Burton was right and Tim was at the ranch.

Connor tried the door, but it was locked. His size twelve boot unlocked it. Once inside, he moved quickly from room to room. The place had two bedrooms, a living room, and a kitchen. It was all one level, no basement. Not many places to hide a seventeen-year-old.

He started in the main bedroom. Tim's dresser was covered with rodeo memorabilia, including several belt buckles the size of Connor's fist. There were also framed advertisements for the rodeo in Cody, Wyoming, and a calendar filled with scantily clad barrel racers. June's model looked fun.

The dresser drawers didn't offer anything interesting, and Connor burned through both bedrooms faster than he thought he would. The US Army had spent a lot of time and money training Connor how to spot things most people would miss, but after scouring Tim's place from top to bottom, he had nothing physical to tie him to Ellie's disappearance. The only items of interest he found were a long-expired milk jug in the refrigerator, an empty trash bag in the garbage can, and a water ring in the toilet. No one had lived here for some time.

The Wyoming Department of Motor Vehicles had registered Tim's F-450 to this address, but that didn't mean it was his full-time residence. Officer Burton mentioned Tim was a ranch hand. Maybe he was living there.

17

BEWARE THE DARKNESS

ELLIE DIDN'T KNOW how long they'd been sitting there. It could have been two hours or ten. Her eyes were open but she was in a fog, someplace between asleep and awake. The sound of the metal bar jarred her back to the moment. Someone, she assumed Little John, was working the bar across the door. She turned to Regan, who was already wide-eyed. The tense muscles in her leg indicated she was ready to go.

"Remember, it's him or us," said Ellie. "We don't stop until it's done. You keep swinging that thing until his knees are Jell-O or it breaks apart in your hand."

"I'm ready," said Regan.

Ellie didn't doubt her.

As the door opened, Ellie felt the rough zipper between her thumb and index finger. Little John stepped into the room carrying two trays. The first time he delivered lunch after Ellie arrived, he ordered everyone to stand at the back of the room. She wondered if he would do that again. The outcome of the next few seconds wouldn't change even if he did.

To Ellie's surprise, he didn't order them back. He also made no mention of the sleeping bag draped over the toilet. Either he didn't notice or he didn't care.

As Little John knelt and placed the two trays on the floor, Ellie's leg muscles tightened, like a rattlesnake ready to strike. He slid the trays toward the girls and began to stand. Ellie was the first to lunge. Before he realized what was happening, she was on him. She wrapped the nylon cord around his neck and pulled as hard as she could. Little John was already off balance, and it didn't take much effort to drag him to the concrete floor.

It all happened so fast that Ellie wasn't sure if he screamed of not. She knew that once she cut off his airway it wouldn't take long before he was unconscious. Her father had made her watch a self defense video when she turned sixteen. She'd forgotten most of it, but remembered the part about cutting off the airway of an attacker and that it didn't take much effort to constrict the carotid artery in the neck. The video made a big deal about it being easy for a smaller person to subdue a much larger person from behind. It was frightening and empowering at the same time. The key was getting into the right position. And Ellie was in the right position. She'd made sure of that.

Little John gurgled and Ellie pulled even tighter, as if trying to take his head clean off. Regan moved just as fast. She whipped the sleeping bag off of the porcelain toilet lid, picked it up, and went to work.

Regan tried to line up her shot, but Little John's feet slipped and skittered on the concrete floor, making it hard for her to zero in. Her first swing glanced off the side of Little John's calf. He likely didn't feel that, but Ellie would bet he felt the next one. That one smashed into his left knee. It must have shattered.

Little John thrashed violently and it took everything Ellie had to hang on. She remembered her instructions to Regan.

We've got to commit. It's him or us.

Regan's third strike did the most damage. Ellie felt the bones in his leg snap, as the vibrations ran up his torso. A moment later, she felt Little John slump over, his muscles relaxing. She held on and pulled even tighter and began counting. When she hit thirty, she released her grip. The color rushed back into her hands as she stepped away, leaving Little John unconscious on the floor.

"Is he dead," asked Regan, backing away.

"I don't know." Ellie had never seen a dead person outside of a funeral home. She couldn't tell if Little John was breathing or not. She thought about checking for a pulse, but then realized she didn't care.

"We gotta go," said Ellie. She stuffed the zipper into her pocket, knelt, and slid her hand inside one of Little John's pockets. She thought she felt his thigh move as she fished around inside. Nothing. She searched his other pocket, and that's when she found it. A keyring with two keys. She stood and ran through the doorway. Stopping on the other side, she examined the bar lock on the heavy wooden door. Regan watched, still holding the toilet tank lid with both hands.

Ellie jerked on the bar, working it back and forth. It squeaked and groaned, but after a few seconds of effort, she pulled the bar free from the door. She wondered if anyone was paying attention to the time Little John had been downstairs. How long before they came looking for him? Maybe he was the only one on watch. No way to know.

The girls sprinted down the hall, past the shower and the other doors until they arrived at the door at the end of the hallway. Ellie looked down and saw the keyhole just above the handle. She grabbed the keyring, but Regan snatched it from her hand and forced it into the lock.

She turned the key, but something wasn't right. She tried again.

"It's not lining up," she said.

Again, she forced it.

Ellie swallowed a breath as the key snapped in half, plugging the lock with a jagged shard of metal.

"No!" screamed Regan. "Fuck!"

Ellie pinched the broken end of the key and tried to turn it in the lock, already knowing she couldn't.

"What are we going to do now?" asked Regan.

"Let me think." Ellie examined the door. She grabbed the handle and pulled. It was locked, but it was loose. She tried again, mustering some untapped strength she kept in reserve somewhere. It rattled again but still didn't open.

"We're trapped," said Regan.

Ellie looked down at the rod in her hand and then up at the door. The hinges. They were worn and rusted. She pressed the end of the rod against the top hinge pin and slid her hands a foot or so from the other end of the rod.

"Knock 'em out," she said.

Regan tapped the lid against the rod. Each time she hit it, the girls watched the hinge pin rise another half inch until, finally, it jumped from the hinge and fell to their feet.

"What about the lower one?" said Regan. "The bar won't fit underneath it."

Ellie was already on it. Without the pin, the top of

the door was coming away from the doorframe. She jammed the rod between the top of the door and the frame and pried. She pulled with everything she had until the door separated enough that Regan could slip two hands along the side and join in. Together, they pulled the door inward until its weight snapped the lower hinge clear off the frame. The door fell at their feet like some large tree.

Regan grabbed the toilet tank lid and they stepped over the collapsed door and into a completely dark room.

"What's this?" asked Regan. "I can't see a thing." She stumbled forward, but Ellie steadied her.

"Steps." She remembered back to her arrival. She had counted everything. "Six of them. The lights must be out."

"Six steps?"

"Right. And then there's a hallway. It's longer than the one outside our room. Maybe twice as long? Three times? I don't know. It seemed like it went on forever."

Ellie looped her arm around Regan's and they carefully took the steps, counting each as they went. When they reached the sixth step, Ellie put an arm out to feel for anything, but only found darkness. She took small steps, still entwined with Regan.

"It's the hallway," she said.

"What's at the other end?"

"Another door, then ten steps, and then we're out."

Ellie searched the darkness for the wall. Once she found it, the girls moved arm in arm down the hallway completely blind. Ellie waited for a burst of light to cut through the darkness as someone opened the door at the other end and came rushing in, no doubt convinced something had happened to Little John. She was surprised when reinforcements didn't come.

As they moved forward, Ellie's heart thumped in her chest. The sensation had likely been there all along, but she had only now noticed it in the silence and blackness.

"We've got to be close," she said, breaking the stillness.

"The door up ahead, is it locked?"

"Yes, but it should be locked from the inside. Whoever bought me down used a key to open it. I think it's a deadbolt, so there's got to be a mechanism on this side."

A few more steps and Ellie's hand found a corner. She jerked on Regan's arm to keep her from walking face-first into the door.

"We're here," said Ellie, feeling along the door for the deadbolt. It didn't take long to find. A simple knob. She turned it and both girls pushed the door open. Ellie had expected blinding sunlight, but it didn't come. Instead, a million stars welcomed them into the final, open-air stairwell.

"Oh my God," said Regan, letting the porcelain lid fall to the floor. "Let's go."

They charged up the remaining steps and out onto the dirt ground.

Ellie looked around. A house and several outbuildings about a hundred yards out were illuminated by the moonlight. It was a ranch. Several rooms were lit and Ellie wondered how many people were in there. When she saw a porch light switch on, she grabbed Regan and tore off in the opposite direction of the house. They ran, not stopping, until both were so out of breath they collapsed on the dusty ground.

18

IT'S HIM OR US

OFFICER BURTON WAS ABOUT to leave for the night when Chief Hatson sat down in the chair across from his desk. He repositioned his duty belt when the butt of his revolver pressed into his hip.

"We need to talk," said the chief.

"What's up?"

"I just got off the phone with Ken McMurphy. He said you stopped by the Pale Horse Ranch to talk to Tim Waters."

"That's right. Just had a few questions."

"About what exactly?"

"About that accident Connor Harding mentioned. About the damage to Tim's truck."

"Why are you talking to Tim about that? He's not a suspect in anything."

Burton swallowed hard. He knew he was being squeezed between Harding and Chief Hatson, and he chose his words carefully.

"I was keeping an eye on Tim's place when Harding

showed up. Just like you asked me to do. Harding was hell-bent on talking to Tim about that accident. I figured it would be better if *I* talked to him instead. Thought it was a good way to diffuse the situation."

"I'm gonna stop you right there, son." He adjusted his belt again. "I know you're new around here, but we don't take direction from civilians. You take orders from me and Sergeant Hatson, not some outsider from wherever. We clear?"

"Yessir. I just figured—"

"You don't need to be figuring nothing. And you sure as hell don't need to be implicating Tim Waters in some nonexistent crime. Ken McMurphy is one of Big Rock's best citizens, and he's right-pissed that you showed up to talk to his ranch hand. What do you think the other hands are going to say? They're going to think he's in some sort of trouble."

Burton shifted in his seat. "I just wanted to inquire about the accident. It was just a few questions."

"And what did he say?"

"Tim said there was an accident at the ranch. Said McMurphy would back him up."

"Yeah, that sounds about right. Sounds much more realistic than a hit-and-run and child abduction, don't it?"

"Yessir. It's just that something doesn't sit right."

"And what's that?"

"If Ellie Armstrong isn't missing, then where is she?"

"Who knows where she is? Maybe she's with a friend, with another relative. A boyfriend, maybe. Who knows? There's no evidence she's missing at all. I talked to the EMTs who responded to that accident, and they said there was no one else in that car when it went off the road. They said the driver was pretty banged up. If there was someone else in the car, they'd be banged up too."

"Maybe she was disorientated and wandered away and got lost out there."

"Not likely. I think the more obvious thing is that she's fine and this Harding person is beating a bunch of bushes trying to find something that isn't there. He's blinded by this idea of a hit-and-run. Can't accept another explanation."

"Chief, I get that Harding is bad news. I can tell. He's going to torch the town looking for this girl, whether she's really missing or not. I figured if we could help him out and send him on his way, there's less chance he's going to cause a real problem. You should have seen him. He was ready to tear Tim's head off if he found him."

"You leave Harding to me. If he starts stirring up shit in my town, I'll deal with him, and he ain't going to like that one bit." Chief Hatson stood up. "Now listen. You stay away from the Pale Mare Ranch. If there's a reason to go up there, I'll go talk to McMurphy. We clear?"

Burton hesitated.

"I said are we clear?"

"Clear, Chief."

"We got to take care of our own around here, son. When that so-called missing girl shows up, this Harding fella is going to leave Big Rock. But you, me and Sergeant Hatson are still gonna be here. And so is everyone else in this town. We're one community and we need to stick together. You understand what I'm saying?"

Burton nodded.

"Tim Waters is a hard worker, a good man. I've known him since he and Willie were kids. We go way back. But Harding? He's temporary. Big Rock isn't. So if you want keep wearing that badge, I need you on our side stand'n next to *us*, not Connor Harding. You understand?"

"I understand, Chief."

19

A WILD NIGHT AT THE HUNTING LODGE

GINNY SAID they were running prostitution out of the Hunting Lodge. Working girls were always a reliable source of information. They seemed to know everything about certain people, and they talked to one another. They discussed who the best tippers were, who liked to play a little too rough, who had the best pills, and who was most likely to put a knife to your throat. It was self-preservation. Connor wanted to tap into that resource and see if someone knew anything about Ellie.

Even though it was a good sixty miles from Big Rock, The Hunting Lodge was easy to find following Ginny's directions. A left out of the Frontier Inn's parking lot, then a cool hour's drive until mile marker 167. Just off the exit, the bar stood like an oasis for anyone looking to pass the time with a beer, a woman, or anything else.

The outside was plain, its red and white siding having faded under decades of the sweltering Wyoming sun. Connor could see the cracked and broken slats even in the moonlight. Behind the main building was a smaller structure, which had six doors. Connor assumed they were entrances to small bedrooms. From a distance, the "bays" reminded him of Milner's body shop, but instead of automotive repairs, the patrons here were getting a different type of body work.

A barback carrying a bucket of something exited a rear door, and Connor took the opportunity to slip into the kitchen. He followed the trail of black rubber non-slip mats past a freezer and a three-compartment sink. Beyond that, he walked through a door and found himself staring at a stuffed grizzly bear about nine-feet tall. It was roped off in the corner of the bar, and part of one leg was missing, as if some other animal had taken a bite out of it.

With a name like The Hunting Lodge, Connor expected to see walls lined with stuffed animal heads, maybe bison, antelope, and a turkey or two. He was disappointed when he only found the once majestic grizzly, now deteriorating under the bored gazes of the bar's patrons.

The Hunting Lodge had two long bars spanning opposite walls. There were a dozen barstools at each, maybe half of which were occupied. The center of the room was a haphazard arrangement of tables of varying sizes and four pool tables. Several booths lined the back wall and at the far end was a jukebox, which belted out a country song Connor couldn't identify.

The place wasn't packed, but it wasn't dead either. There were more people than Connor thought there should be out here in the middle of nowhere. While he estimated forty-some faces in the crowd, he only recognized one. At a corner table sat Sergeant Hatson, who had exchanged his tan uniform for a black-and-red flannel shirt and jeans. Flanking him sat two bearded men who took their denim seriously. All three eyeballed him as he walked across the peanut shell-littered floor and sat down across from them.

"What the hell you doing here?" asked Hatson. "Thought you were working."

"A man can't get a drink?"

Hatson lifted a bottle to his lips, and Connor felt the other two men sizing him up. Hatson's friends could pass for twins in the right light. One was slightly taller with his hair pulled back in a ponytail, while the other had a tight buzzcut.

"You think you're going to find your missing girl here?"

"I hope not," said Connor. "I'd hope an upstanding place like this wouldn't cater to underage girls."

"It don't." Hatson cracked a peanut shell between his fingers. "Officer Burton working for you now?"

"No."

"Heard he's been snooping around asking questions. The kind of questions you're asking. You're liable to get him in some trouble."

"Sounds like he's just doing his job. You should pay attention. Might learn something from him."

"Tim Waters and I go way back. I already talked to him. He's not involved in any hit-and-run. Or anything else for that matter."

"How do you explain the damage to his truck?"

"You mean the illegally searched truck? He said there was an accident at the ranch. Happens from time to time. Let it go, Harding. Tim is a hardworking and honest man. If he says he's not involved, then I believe him."

"The evidence says otherwise."

"Like I said, it was an accident at the ranch."

"Which is why it was hidden in Milner's personal garage? I don't buy it."

Hatson grabbed another handful of peanuts and began shelling them.

"You should probably get a move on. Not smart to go poking bears around here."

"I came to Big Rock to find Ellie Armstrong, and I'm not leaving until I find her. You and Tim Waters should know that."

"I'd advise against making threats like that. I hear you're already ruffling some feathers. Tim said someone kicked in the door to his home. You know something about that?"

"Not a thing."

"First, Milner's and now Tim's place? You're starting to piss off the wrong people. You keep pushing, someone's liable to push back."

"Fine with me."

Across the room, a woman in a short skirt and tank top walked up to the bar and handed something to the bartender. It was the woman Connor was there to see, even though she didn't know it.

"Enjoy your drinks, fellas." He stood up. "I'll be seeing you."

"You know, the desert's a dangerous place," said Hatson. "Lots of trouble to get into. Lots of places to disappear."

"I hope someone's stupid enough to try. And I really hope that person is you. So far, you've seen the nice side of me, Hatson. You don't want to see the other side."

Connor made his way to the bar, feeling eyes on his back the entire way. He took the stool next to the woman in the miniskirt. He hoped she could offer some news about Ellie, had maybe heard something through the working girl grapevine.

She eyeballed him, took a cigarette from her clutch purse, and torched it. Her straight cotton-white hair reached her shoulders. It framed her face perfectly, draping over her ears and curving beneath her pink lips like a chin strap. Her white tank top was failing miserably at its job. Connor glanced down at her pink skirt. It that looked more like a headband than a piece of clothing. He thought she looked like a character out of a sci-fi magazine he read as a kid. Some sexy astronaut with a fishbowl over her head and a laser gun in her hand kicking ass across the galaxy.

She rubbed the back of her neck, took a long draw off her cigarette, and waited for Connor to speak first.

"You on the clock?" asked Connor.

"Maybe," she said, taking another long drag.

"What's your name?"

"Holly."

He waited for Holly to ask his name, but she wasn't interested.

"So how does this work?"

"Well, you can pay by the drink or by the hour, sweetheart. If you buy me a drink, then we sit here at the bar. If you take the hour, you pay the bartender a hundo and we go to the back. Dealer's choice."

He wanted conversation, but the bar was too public. Standing up, he slipped a hundred-dollar bill from his wallet and set it on the bar.

Holly knocked on the bar twice and the bartender came over, slipped the bill into his pocket, and wrote something down on a notepad.

"Number four," he said.

Holly stood up, took Connor's hand, and led him out a side door. They walked behind the bar to the row of units Connor had seen earlier. She opened the door to unit four, crushed out the cigarette on the doorframe, and led him inside.

The room wasn't much larger than a jail cell, with just a bed, a nightstand, and two chairs. A bathroom with a shower was at the back of the room. The accommodations made the Frontier Inn look like the Plaza Hotel.

Holly opened the nightstand drawer and tossed a condom on the bed.

"We can do whatever you want, but any freaky shit is gonna cost extra. And no choking or hitting." She started pulling down her skirt.

Connor was surprised she needed the disclaimer.

"I'm not here for freaky shit. Just information."

"Oh, fuck off, you twat."

She repositioned the pink mini and started toward the door, but Connor blocked it.

"I'll make it worth your time," he said.

She stepped back and sized him up. "How's that?"

"What do you make in a night?"

"What?"

"What do you pull in each night?"

"After the house cut, something like four hundred on a weekend. Why?"

"I've got some questions about a missing girl. Give me some info that will help me and I'll double your nightly take."

"You're going to give me eight hundred bucks?"

"Yeah, and all you have to do is talk. It'll be the easiest money you'll make at this job."

"Okay." She sat on one of the chairs, crossed her legs, and tossed the white wig onto the bed, revealing short brown hair. "Shoot then."

"I'm looking for a seventeen-year-old. Name's Ellie. She's rail thin with blue hair, just past her shoulders." He slipped his phone from his pocket, pulled up her photo, and held it in front of Holly. "You ever see her around here?"

"No, and I'd remember seeing someone with blue hair, that's for sure."

"She lives in Big Rock," added Connor.

"Well, there's your problem. If she lives in Big Rock, she's probably not missing at all. More likely she ran off. To get out of Big Rock."

"I don't think so. She's not the type to do that."

"Okay, so she just up and vanished?"

"She was in an auto accident with her father. Pops ended up in the hospital, but there's no trace of the girl. I think someone intentionally ran him off the road and then took the girl. You know anyone who might do something like that?"

"Look, there's some shady stuff that happens out here, but kidnapping? That's nothing I've ever heard of."

"What about the girls who work here, where do they come from?"

"Honey, this ain't no destination. No woman comes here. This is the kind of place where you *end up*."

"Anyone working here against their will? Got tricked into coming out here? Pressured into working off some debt or something?"

"No, all the women here are legit. It's all on the up-and-up. I mean, it's as legit as possible for a cathouse, right? I'd know if someone was being kept here against their will. I'm not saying any of us *want* to be here, but no one is forcing us to stay."

Connor thought about Sergeant Hatson guzzling beer with his two friends. "You know Sergeant Hatson?"

"Yeah. I saw you talking to him in the bar. You two friends or something?"

"No. Quite the opposite. I've been trying to get him to look into Ellie's disappearance, but he's not interested. He's not too keen of a police officer. That's a big red flag for me."

"Willie Hatson is about as good a cop as I am. He comes in and shakes us down from time to time. Wants a tug job to look the other way, that sort of thing. I always figured he was getting some sort of kickback for all this, but, you now, it's not like I get to look at the books."

"He involved in anything? Sergeant Hatson?"

"Years ago, there was a big drug bust in Casper. Heroin and meth, I think. Like a big-time operation that the DEA broke up. Made the news and everything. There were rumors Willie and his dad were involved. Not like big players or anything, but that they were involved in getting drugs to Casper. Or maybe it was getting it out of Casper, I don't remember. They never got wrapped up in the bust, so maybe those were just rumors. I'm sure he's crooked as shit, but I don't know what he's into." She looked Connor up and down again. "You really going to pay me eight hundred bucks?"

Connor slipped out his wallet, counted out eight hundred-dollar bills, and set them on the mattress. "Drug runners, huh? I thought you were going to say Willie and his father owned this joint."

"I doubt they'd know what to do with it. No, McMurphy owns this place. Has for years."

"McMurphy?"

"Ken McMurphy. Big deal around here. Owns the Pale Mare Ranch. It's massive. Breeds horses and sells them to other ranches all over the country."

"Ken McMurphy. Thanks, that's helpful."

"You know, when you first said you were looking for a missing girl, I figured you were looking into that Indian girl."

"She's come up a few times. Know anything about her?"

She shook her head. "Just as much as anyone else. The FBI came out here and talked to people about it. Not me, but some of the other girls."

"They learn anything useful?"

Holly thought for a moment and fluffed her hair. "Don't know. I don't think they found her. Never heard anything if they did. If someone did snatch her, she'd be long gone by now."

"Thanks, Holly." Connor stood up. "You've been helpful."

"I can talk to some of the other girls and see if they know anything about your blue-haired friend, but we all talk, like all the time, and I think that would have come up."

"You got a phone?"

"Of course." Holly slipped her phone from her clutch.

Connor rattled off his phone number as she typed in the digits.

"It's going to look suspicious if we walk out of here after only fifteen minutes. You paid for an hour. Want to use the rest of the time? I can put the wig back on."

"I appreciate the offer, but I have to get back to Big Rock. Might stop by the Pale Mare Ranch."

"Suit yourself."

Connor walked out of the room and headed back to his truck. When he reached the parking lot, he heard two car doors open and then slam shut. A moment later, Sergeant Hatson's denim-clad friends emerged from the darkness. Hatson was nowhere in sight.

Connor's forty-five was back at the Frontier Inn, and while he wasn't looking for a fight, apparently one was looking for him.

He waited for the men to speak, but they didn't. Their body language did the talking for them. They stood broad shouldered, trying to look larger than they were. Both wore obscenely large belt buckles like the ones Connor saw in Tim's house. He made a mental note not to punch too low or risk breaking a hand on the metal.

"Well, come on then," said Connor. "Best to get this over with. I've got shit to do."

Connor looked past the men hoping for a glimpse of Hatson. Maybe his ploy was to orchestrate a fight, only to haul Connor in on some bogus assault charge. That wasn't going to happen. Connor had heard too many stories about small-town police justice. He wasn't going to let anyone arrest him because he knew he'd never make it back to the station. He'd more likely disappear in the desert just like Hatson said.

The larger of the two men stepped forward. Connor raised his fists in a traditional boxing stance. He was good in a fight. The key was to end it fast while inflicting as much damage as possible, and that's what he aimed to do. The big fella, the one with the ponytail, circled behind him. Connor stepped around to his right until both men were in front of him again. He kept them in line with one another. He'd deal with them one at a time, from the front.

Ponytail surged forward. He was looking to use his weight to take the fight to the ground. Connor sidestepped to the left and watched the man go by, then realigned himself, putting both men in front again. Connor would let him do this all night if that was his play. A few more lunges and the big man would be winded. Ponytail must have realized that too, because after another failed attempt, he stood up straight and mirrored Connor's boxer's stance. After a moment of thought, he shifted his weight to his rear and dropped his right shoulder. It was a slight movement, but it told Connor everything he needed to know. Never telegraph a punch. As the big man swung a hard right at Connor's head, he ducked under the flying fist and delivered a solid left hand to Ponytail's ribs. They cracked under the force of his knuckles. As Ponytail heaved forward, Connor drove his boot into the man's left knee, shattering it. Two quick right hands to his head, and the big man was unconscious on the pavement.

Connor had hoped that by dispatching the first so quickly his friend might reconsider his options and call it a night. That didn't happen. Buzzcut slipped a knife from his boot and started toward him. Connor wasn't about to take his chances with a blade. As buzzcut moved forward, Connor backed away toward a row of vehicles. He turned and ran down the line, stopping at the first pickup he could find. Keeping an eye on the man with the knife, he looked inside the tuck's bed for anything he could use. He'd reached the third truck before he found something of value, a crowbar.

He doubled back to his truck, content to leave Buzzcut in the parking lot, but the man with the blade slipped out from behind another vehicle, positioning himself between Connor and his rental.

This time, Connor was ready. He moved calmly forward, keeping the crowbar in front of him. The smart move was to use the tool to keep as much distance as possible between his vital organs and the blade. Connor knew that right-handed knife attacks come from one of three directions: from overhead, blade angled down, *Psycho*-style; a slash across the body from left to right; or a thrusting motion, the knife outstretched in front of the attacker. He waited for the man's body position to reveal his move, and after a few moments it did. Buzzcut turned the blade in his hand so it was facing down, stepped forward, and raised it overhead, preparing to thrust downward. He wouldn't get the chance. As soon as his arm went up, Connor lunged forward, looking more like a fencer than a boxer, and drove the crowbar's curved end into the man's sternum. The force knocked him backward into Connor's truck, where he fell to the pavement. Everyone has a plan until they take a crowbar to the chest.

Disorientated, Buzzcut tried to get to his feet, but Connor was too fast. He drove his boot into man's jaw, snapping his head back into the truck's footstep. He slumped to the pavement unconscious, the knife still in his hand.

Connor checked behind him and saw Ponytail, now conscious, crawling toward the bar. After pulling Buzzcut out of the way, he pocketed the knife, climbed into the pickup, kicked it into gear, and rolled out of the parking lot.

• • •

Sergeant Hatson pulled into his driveway as his cell phone rang. He recognized the number.

"What do you need, McMurphy?"

"We've got a problem. The two girls escaped."

"What? How?"

"Never mind how. I need you to get out there and look for them."

"Why me?"

"Because if they reach civilization, we're all fucked. I've got my people on it too, but I need all hands on deck. Find them."

"Which direction are they headed?"

"I don't know. Get over here and we'll talk through a plan."

"I'm on my way."

20

ON THE RUN

WHEN CONNOR WOKE up the next morning, his knuckles were already swollen. He stepped into the office to find Ginny asleep behind the counter, a television blaring an episode of some gameshow from the 1980s.

"Morning!" He slammed his fist on the counter.

Ginny shot up, almost tipping her chair.

"For shit's sake. What the hell?"

"You know anything about Ken McMurphy?"

Ginny muted the television. "Who?"

"Ken McMurphy. He owns The Hunting Lodge."

"And just about everything else," said Ginny.

"What do you know about him?"

"He's a huge landowner around here. Has a ranch that breeds and sells horses. Why?"

"That ranch he owns, the Pale Mare, that's the same one where Tim Waters works."

"So?"

"That's one hell of a coincidence."

"Maybe, but look around. In case you haven't noticed,

Big Rock isn't the center of industry. There aren't too many employment opportunities around here. The Pale Mare probably employs half the town." She rubbed her head and reached for her coffee cup. "And what would he have to do with your missing girl?"

"Maybe nothing. Or maybe something. I didn't find anything at Tim's home, and it doesn't look like he lives there anymore. Figured he was living at the ranch instead. And if that's the case, maybe there's something going on there."

"I don't know. McMurphy seems like an upstanding guy. Pillar of the community type."

"Sometimes those are the ones you have to look out for." Connor was about to leave when something caught his eye. "What are the binoculars for?"

"They're good for seeing things that are far away," said Ginny.

"Funny. Can I borrow them?"

She handed them across the counter. "You going to the ranch now?"

"No, I'll go tonight after the sun goes down."

"That can be good. And why do I have a bad feeling I'm not going to get those back in one piece?"

"I'll do what I can. Now, how do I get to the ranch?"

Ellie didn't know how far they had run or how long they'd slept, but when she and Regan woke, the sun was beating down on them. A sharp pain engulfed Ellie's feet as soon as she stood up, and for the first time, she realized she wasn't wearing any shoes. They were probably back at the ranch with her purse and cell phone. What she wouldn't give for those sneakers now.

Regan stirred and sat up, rubbing the bottom of her bare foot. She plucked a twig from her sole and tossed it aside. "How far do you think we ran?"

"Don't know. Had to be a few miles. At least."

"I didn't think I could run that far," said Regan. "Barefoot no less."

"Me neither. Only problem is I don't know what direction we went. No clue where we are." Ellie slowly turned, taking in the landscape.

They were in a field underneath a deep, ocean-blue sky with a scatter of clouds. The grass was as brown as a wheat field, and except for the few hills that the ground coughed up, the terrain was as flat as a dollar bill.

"Wherever we are, it's better than back there," said Regan.

"Agreed, but we need to find some water. Shelter too, if possible."

"Do you think they'll be looking for us."

"I'd bet on it. I don't think they can risk us getting away and finding our way back to town to the police."

"What would we even tell the police? I don't know where we were. Sure as hell couldn't describe it."

"Me neither. That house, it was too dark. Maybe they have those mugshot books, like on TV. We could look though those and see if Little John or Anchorman are in there. We're getting ahead of ourselves though. First thing we have to do is keep moving. They might not know what direction we went in, but they're probably already looking for us."

"There's nothing out here. Where do we go?"

Ellie knew a bit about surviving in the outdoors, but until now, she'd never been tested.

"Water and shade," she said.

"What?"

"This sun is going to bake us. We've got to find shade and water. Otherwise, we're going to be in trouble real quick."

"What about food?"

"That can wait. Water is more important."

Regan shielded the sun from her eyes and looked in every direction. "Is there even water out here?"

"Hope so."

"You said you were from Big Rock, Wyoming, right?" asked Regan. "Any idea how far we are from there?"

"No. I was unconscious when they brought me to that hellhole. Could be two miles or two hundred. I don't know."

"But you think we're still in Wyoming?"

"I think so." Ellie drew in a deep breath. "Sure smells like it."

"What's the plan then?"

"Let's see how far we can get before it gets too hot. Keep an eye out for anything we can use for shelter." Ellie pointed to what she thought was east. "Let's get under that cloud cover. We'll walk with the clouds, try to stay in the shade."

Regan looked around as they began walking. "This looks like the kind of place you see in horror movies, where your car breaks down in the middle of nowhere. The kind of place where people die."

"People do die out here, but not us."

. . .

Ellie figured they'd walked for several hours, but they still hadn't seen any sign of water or anything else.

"Is that a fence?"

Ellie stopped. "What?"

"A fence." Regan pointed toward the horizon. "Am I seeing things? It looks like a fence."

Ellie wiped her eyes and focused. "I think it *is* a fence. Maybe our luck is turning around."

"Why is that lucky?"

"If there's a fence, then there's something to fence in. Cattle maybe. And if there's cattle, then there's likely a water source. Ranchers move their cattle from field to field, but they usually fence in areas near natural water sources. Animals gotta drink too."

Ellie looked up and realized heading toward the fence would take them out from under the clouds. They'd be walking in the direct sun, and they didn't know for how long.

It seemed like another hour passed before they made it to the fence. When they reached it, Ellie wrapped her hands around the rough, cracked timbers to hold herself up. She tried to remember the last time she'd had a drink of anything. She knew food wasn't an issue, as people could live for a month or more before starving to death. Lack of water and rapid temperature drops at night were the immediate threats. Out here, either one could get you.

The fence was a standard ranch fence. The timbers were arranged like the letter A with a horizontal beam running across the top and then two other beams, one on each side, below that. Ellie looked out and couldn't see an end to the fence line. Just one section after the other, rinse and repeat.

The girls slipped through the beams, and while the other side looked the same, it brought a minor sense of optimism. The fence meant civilization, maybe even people. People who could help them.

"If there's a fence, does that mean there's a ranch?" said Regan.

"Not necessarily. Could just be a field, but there may be an outbuilding or something. Ranchers sometimes keep basic supplies out here. It's not for long-term living though."

"Gotcha."

"But maybe we get lucky and there's a luxury ranch with AC on full blast," said Ellie. "Gotta think positive."

Ellie figured it was another hour before they saw the cow. It was solid brown and likely saw them before they saw it. It didn't seem to care they were there, focusing instead on the large swatch of grass it was eating. After they passed the first cow, others started to appear. They emerged one after the other, like stars in the early night sky.

"Are they dangerous?" asked Regan.

"Not really, but don't get too close just in case. You don't want one of these gals knocking you over."

Ellie scanned the area. There had to be water nearby, but it wasn't going to be a raging river. It was going to be a small spring or some other pocket of water that might not even be visible until you were standing on top of it.

The girls kept moving through the field. Ellie was about to stop to rest when she saw a group of about ten cows standing together with their heads down.

"There," she shouted. "It's got to be water. Let's go!"

Ellie began running, surprised that her legs could move that fast. Regan was only a few steps behind her. They closed the distance and arrived next to the cows who, like the others, didn't seem to care the girls were there. Ellie looked down to see a narrow brook about a foot wide snaking through the field. She fell to her knees, cupped her hands, and began to drink. The water was lukewarm, but she swore it was the coldest thing to cross her lips in a long time.

The girls were still sitting next to the cows, drinking water out of their hands, when the wind began to blow.

21

THE PALE MARE RANCH

Connor followed Ginny's directions to McMurphy's ranch. A strong wind pelted the windshield of his rental with dust and small rocks. After passing the entrance gate, he drove another half mile and pulled off the road, parking far enough in the brush that any passing headlights wouldn't find the rental. He snatched the binoculars from the passenger seat and started walking back to the ranch.

Connor didn't know what he expected to find there, maybe nothing. Tim's involvement in the hit-and-run and his connection to the ranch could be a coincidence, but he owed it to Aiden and Ellie to find out. He needed proof, and this was his chance. The plan was simple—observe. Connor didn't know a thing about ranches, other than this particular ranch bred and sold horses. He'd observe from a distance and watch the place for the night. Were trucks coming in and out at peculiar times? Was there a security detail? Was there anything happening that shouldn't be? Any checkmarks and he'd go in for a closer look.

Surveying the terrain, he noticed a hill overlooking the

front of the ranch. He'd set up there and spend a few hours squinting through Ginny's binoculars, hoping the moon provided enough light to see through them. Then he'd move around the perimeter and eventually scout the place from all sides. He was halfway up the hill when three small rocks rolled down from the top. He stopped his advance, crouched and put the lenses to his face. The moon illuminated the hill just enough for him to see someone lying down facing the ranch.

The wind picked up again and Connor covered his eyes as his face was pelted with pebbles and small debris from the hillside. He moved closer, being careful where he stepped. Once he made it halfway up the hill, he stopped again. It was still too dark to make out any specific features, other than whoever was at the top of the hill was lying on his chest and wearing what looked like desert camo hunting gear.

Continuing his advance, Connor took each step deliberately, knowing the wrong move could give away his position. The howling wind helped conceal his movement, but he was still careful not to step on anything that could alert someone to his presence.

When he reached the top of the hill, he saw the man was propped up on his elbows, peering through his own binoculars. A few more steps and he was only a few feet away. The camo-clad trespasser must have heard him, because he rolled onto his side, reached for something, and tried to stand. Connor lunged forward, secured the man's wrist and pressed his other hand over his mouth. There, looking back at him with wide, terror-filled eyes was Officer Kyle Burton.

"You got a warrant for this surveillance?" asked Connor, removing his hand.

"Fucking Christ. You scared the hell out of me. What are you doing here?"

"I was about to ask you the same thing."

"Just checking up on things," said Burton, going back to his binoculars.

Connor lay down next to him and peered through Ginny's binoculars.

The ranch was mostly quiet. Connor observed two men whom he assumed were ranch hands moving boxes out the front door and carrying them to a barn about fifty yards from the main house. Scanning the property, Connor looked for anything out of the ordinary. So far, he didn't see anything that piqued his interest.

"What did you find out when you talked to Tim?"

"Not much," said Burton. "Said there was an accident at the ranch, which is how he busted up his truck."

"You believe him?"

"I'm here aren't I?"

"Yeah, you are," said Connor, pushing a rock out from under his thigh. "And why are you here?"

"You know how when someone tells you not to do something, it just makes you want to do it more? Well, the chief told me to back off Tim Waters. He didn't like me talking to him. Made me think something was going on."

"You see anything here tonight that confirms that?"

"Not yet." He set the binoculars on the ground and rubbed his eyes. "What did you find at Tim's place?"

"You said not to go inside Tim's place, or you'd, I think you said, 'haul me in.'"

"You don't seem like the kind of person who would listen to me."

"I didn't."

"So, what did you find?"

"Nothing, but it didn't look like he lives there." Connor scanned the property again looking for a bunkhouse. "Figured he's living here."

"You're probably right."

Connor set the binoculars down and repositioned himself. When he turned on his side to remove another rock from under his leg, he noticed a patch on Burton's shoulder. The shield-shaped insignia was dull yellow with a green diagonal band and white buffalo skull.

"You military?" said Connor, tapping the patch.

"Montana National Guard," said Burton.

"You wore your fatigues to a stakeout?"

"It was the only camo I had."

"I'm pretty sure that's a violation of the uniform code. Something about not wearing your uniform while off a US or host nation installation while undertaking civilian activities. Uncle Sam might toss you in the brig for that."

"How do you know the uniform code?"

"Because I'm smart enough to know the rules, even if I was dumb enough to enlist."

"You're military?"

"Army Intelligence. Formerly."

"Army Intelligence? What did you do, analyst?"

"Counterintelligence."

"Spy hunter, huh?"

"Something like that. The Army and I decided to part ways a while ago. We split up for the kids."

A pair of headlights caught Connor's attention, and he

snapped the binoculars back to his eyes and tracked the vehicle. Not surprisingly, it was a pickup truck.

"Who do we have here?" said Burton. "Seems pretty late for visitors."

The two men watched as the truck rolled down the dirt driveway.

"That's Sergeant Hatson's truck," said Burton.

The truck parked next to the front door and Hatson stepped out wearing the same jeans and red-and-black flannel Connor had seen him in earlier.

"He must have been out all night. I saw him at The Hunting Lodge last night in the same getup."

"What's he doing here?" said Burton.

"Something is going on, and Hatson is involved."

"That's a leap."

"He sent two men to rough me up last night. I think he's tired of having me around. He's afraid I might find something."

"Two men? How'd that go?"

"Better for me than them." One of the ranch hands opened the front door and Sergeant Hatson stepped inside. "Whose side are you on, Burton?"

"What do you mean?"

"What I mean is I can't get a read on you. One minute you're telling me to stay the hell away and the next we're staking out the same ranch."

"This isn't a stakeout. And I'm not on anyone's side. If there's something going on here, then I want to know about it."

"What if your bosses are involved?"

"I'll cross that bridge when I come to it. Right now, all

we got is Sergeant Hatson visiting the Pale Mare Ranch after hours."

"Way after hours."

"Still, I haven't seen any evidence of anything illegal."

"You're in that office all day long, Burton. You must know something about what they're into."

"I have no idea."

"I heard there was a big drug bust a while ago. Something went down in Casper and the Hatsons may have been running transportation. You know anything about that?"

"If that's true, it was before my time."

"You must have seen something."

"Look, the Hatsons might be too buddy-buddy with McMurphy, but he's one of the biggest landowners in Wyoming. The largest non-government employer too. Anything they're doing is probably more self-serving than illegal."

"Tim Waters is tied into my missing girl, and Tim works for McMurphy, so that's enough to pique my interest in him."

"He's one of the most successful horse ranchers in the country. Why would he have anything to do with a missing girl?"

"I can't shake the FBI connection. I think the hit-and-run was meant to keep him quiet. Maybe he knew something about what was going on around here."

"If that's true, and he was onto something, why not just kill him?"

Connor shook his head. "Put a bullet in his head and the FBI would be all over it. But if he dies in an auto accident, maybe that's just mundane enough not to raise suspicion. Or maybe he wasn't meant to die. Maybe they're holding Ellie somewhere in case he wakes up. An insurance policy."

"But what would Tim or McMurphy be up to that the FBI would be investigating?"

"That's why I'm up here yanking scorpions off of my ass trying to find out."

"This girl's father—"

"Aiden," said Connor.

"Right, Aiden. You said he's a consultant. What does he consult on?"

"I don't know, but I doubt it's horse rustling. One thing's certain, though. If McMurphy's running horses across the country, then he's got one solid distribution operation. He's probably got the trucks to move anything he wants to wherever he wants."

The front door opened, and Connor raised his binoculars back to his eyes. He followed Sergeant Hatson as he walked out the front door and climbed into his truck.

"What kind of guy is this McMurphy?"

"Nice guy as far as I know," said Burton. "He goes into town every Tuesday and Thursday and gets breakfast at Karen's Diner in town. Picks up the tab for everyone there."

"Sounds like a peach."

"I've never heard a bad word about him."

"Well, if he's into something, I'll find out what."

"Where do we go from here?" asked Burton

"Anything that happens next is going to violate someone's civil rights, so it's best you aren't involved. Plus, I could use you at the station keeping your ears up. If Hatson sent someone after me, I must be getting close, even if I don't know exactly what I'm getting close to."

22

___

A TEMPORARY STAY

THE SUN HAD SET hours ago and it was a welcome relief. Nothing felt as hot as the Wyoming sun. The girls had relished the cloud cover they had the previous afternoon, and they hoped to be as lucky tomorrow. A clear sky, which was as common as a pickup truck in Wyoming, could bake them. Even though they felt fortunate to have found the stream, they yearned now for shelter, something that thus far had eluded them.

Ellie peered off into the distance looking for porch lights. She thought she had found one, and even grabbed Regan's arm to show her, but the elation quickly faded as the two lights moved away from one another.

The girls watched as the lights bounced up and down following the terrain.

"What is that?" said Regan.

"ATVs I think."

They were on the other side of the fence, and whoever was saddled on top of them was in a hurry.

"Let's go," said Regan, running toward the lights.

"Regan, wait!" Elle started after her but tripped on something and went down, her knee cracking into the dusty ground. "Regan!" She sprang back on her feet and went after her, pushing the pain deep somewhere even she didn't know.

Regan stopped at the fence and waved frantically, her arms above her head as if signaling a low-flying plane. Ellie reached her and pulled her down to the ground.

"What are you doing?" said Regan, pushing her away. "Maybe they can help."

"How do you know it's not them? Out looking for us?"

Regan stood back up and continued waving. "How do you know it's not the police or someone else looking for us?"

"The police wouldn't be on ATVs. They'd be in a helicopter. And they'd call off the search at dusk to resume in the morning. And no rancher would be out here after dark. It's them!"

Regan looked at Ellie and then back out at the racing lights. She dropped her arms and sat down in the dirt. "We're going to die out here."

"No, we're not."

"How do you know?"

Ellie thought for a moment. "I know because yesterday, or two days ago, hell, I don't know, we were locked in some lunatic's basement waiting to be sold off to God-knows-who. And now look at us."

"Two beat-to-shit chicks lost in the desert?"

"No, two warriors who strangled and kicked the living fuck out of their captor with a toilet tank lid, broke through two locked doors, and escaped to freedom."

Regan cracked a smile. "I guess that's one way to look at it."

The girls watched as the lights disappeared in the distance.

"Okay," said Regan. "What's the plan then?"

"I think it's best to travel as far as we can at night. We need to limit our time in the sun tomorrow. Even with this stream, we're not going to be able to keep cool enough. We'll find help eventually. We'll find a ranch or a road. And then we can flag down a car. We're going to get out of here, Regan. I promise you that."

The sun was coming up when Regan saw it. At first, they couldn't tell what it was. Some sort of structure off in the distance. In the darkness, they probably would have walked right past it, but the sun was behind it, outlining it in a warm glow that almost looked artificial.

The structure, whatever it was, could have been a mile or more away. Out here, distance, like time, no longer existed. There was just light and dark. But if it was a building, it was exactly what they needed to get out of the approaching sun.

"Let's move," said Regan, breaking into a sprint.

Ellie followed her, not sure where the energy to run came from.

As they got closer, Ellie realized what it was. A toolshed. It was about the size of a single-car garage, and while it was standing, it was in rough shape. Ellie thought even a gentle breeze could flatten it.

The shed had four wooden sides and a tin roof that was coming apart, bending skyward on one side. There were no windows, and the door was leaning off its hinge. Ellie opened the door, careful not the rip it off the shed.

"What in the hell is this?" asked Regan as Ellie stepped inside.

"Rancher's shed."

Inside, the girls found several spools of barbed wire and about two dozen wooden fence posts. There were also a few tools lying about, most rusted beyond use. Ellie had hoped to find some sort of container. The trek to the shed had taken them away from the stream, and she wanted something they could use to carry water with them.

Regan walked to the back of the shed and examined the wooded beams. "What's this doing out here in the middle of nowhere?"

"Must be storage for fence parts. Wonder when the last time was that someone was here."

"Probably before we were born," said Regan.

Regan abandoned the posts and walked to a workbench that spanned one of the sides. She picked up a shovel and jabbed the spade into the dirt floor at her feet.

"Well, at least we can dig our graves when the time comes."

Ellie didn't know why, but she thought that was funny.

23

KAREN'S DINER

CONNOR HAD SLEPT for a few hours in his rental before driving back to Big Rock. He wanted to talk to McMurphy, but the ranch wasn't the place to do it. Burton mentioned McMurphy hit up Karen's Diner in town for breakfast on Tuesdays and Thursdays. If he wasn't there now, he would be soon.

Karen's Diner was in the town square. Connor remembered passing it when he first arrived in Big Rock. Aside from the post office, a hardware store, and a title office, there wasn't much else to see in the center of town. Connor thought back to Boston and the diner where he liked to eat on Saturday mornings. The place was always packed and you often had to wait, sometimes up to a half hour, to get a seat, but the pancakes were worth it. He always ordered the Jackpot Special: two eggs, bacon and a short stack.

He wasn't looking for pancakes today though, just information. And maybe coffee. When Connor stepped inside Karen's Diner, he took a booth in the corner. He ordered a coffee and waited.

He had no idea what Ken McMurphy looked like, but he hadn't seen any Pale Mare Ranch vehicles in the lot, so he sipped his coffee and turned away the waitress each time she returned to the booth with her order pad in hand. Finally, he gave in and ordered the Diner Delight #2, Karen's version of the Jackpot Special. He was thrilled when the plate arrived before McMurphy.

After polishing off the meal, Connor dove into his second cup of coffee as he watched a black pickup truck pull into the lot. He noted the logo on the truck's door—three gold letters, PMR, with a gold lasso around them. It was the same logo from the truck in one of the service bays at Milner's.

A man in his late fifties with slicked back gray hair and a matching mustache stepped out of the vehicle and entered the diner. He sat at a booth on the other side of the diner and received a hug from the same waitress who'd delivered Connor's breakfast.

Connor left a twenty on the table, picked up his coffee, and joined the man at his booth.

"I don't remember requesting a table for two," said the man.

"You Ken McMurphy?"

"That's the rumor. And who are you?"

"Connor Harding."

"Well, Connor Harding, I prefer to eat alone. Is there something I can do for you?"

Connor slid into the booth across from McMurphy. "I'm looking for a missing girl. Ellie Armstrong. Ever hear of her?"

"Yeah, I have. That's the girl Officer Burton was talking

about when he came to my ranch the other day. Talked to one of my ranch hands. I hope he was helpful."

"He was the opposite of helpful."

"Well, I'm sorry to hear that, but it's likely Tim didn't know anything. We deal in horses, not missing people."

"Or he was keeping his mouth shut," said Connor.

McMurphy eased back in his seat. "I'm sorry, are you accusing one of my employees of intentionally lying to the police?"

"I am. I saw Tim Waters's truck at Milner's. One of your other ones too. I know Tim was involved in an accident, a hit-and-run. What I don't know is why."

"There was no hit-and-run. I think we cleared that up with Officer Burton. There was an accident at the ranch. Tim collided with a trailer."

"Head on?" asked Connor.

"Yes. Seems Tim wasn't watching where he was going." McMurphy took a cup of coffee from the waitress and waited for her to leave. "Tim might be an irresponsible driver, but I can assure you there's nothing more to it."

"I think there is."

"Why are you so certain Tim had something to do with this collision?"

"Not a collision, a hit-and-run. The paint transfer on Tim's truck puts him at the scene, and I know Ellie was in the car with her father at the time they went off the road. So that makes Tim the last person to see Ellie."

"So you're accusing Tim of kidnapping now? Hit-and-run and kidnapping?"

"That's right. But what I don't know is why he hit them or where Ellie is now."

"And you think I can shed some light on this?"

"Tim works for you. He lives on your ranch. And you're hiding something. I saw the front of Tim's truck, and that's no trailer accident. You're covering for him, which means you're involved somehow."

"Listen, I'm a rancher. I raise horses. Why would I have anything to do with a hit-and-run or kidnapping?"

"I don't know. But I'll find out."

"I sincerely hope you do. And if there's anything I can do, you let me know."

"I'll tell you what you can do," said Connor. "You can wipe that smug look off your face."

The waitress set a plate of eggs, sausage, and toast next to McMurphy.

"Thanks, dear," he said.

After she walked away, he turned back to Connor. "Look, you're interrupting my meal. I've been rather accommodating with your questions, but I think it's time for you to leave."

Connor stood up and leaned over the table. "You need to understand something, McMurphy. I'm not leaving Big Rock until I find Ellie. I don't care if I have to kick down every door in this town to find her. And there's nothing you or the Hatsons can do about that." He picked up his coffee mug and pressed it into McMurphy's eggs, smearing yellow ooze across the plate, then walked out.

After McMurphy removed the coffee mug and tried to salvage what was left of his breakfast, he picked up his cell phone and dialed. A moment later, Sergeant Hatson answered.

"I just met Connor Harding. You said you were going to take care of that."

"I tried. We ran into a hiccup at The Hunting Lodge."

"Try harder." He hung up the phone.

24

LUCKY BILL TONN

ELLIE HEARD the engine before Regan did. She listened, trying to determine if it was another ATV. Maybe the same ones from the other night.

"Who's that?" said Regan, lifting her head, searching for the source.

Ellie hurried to the front of the shack and peered through a crack in the door.

"Is it them?" asked Regan. "From the ranch?"

"I don't know."

A car door slammed.

"It's not an ATV," said Ellie as she turned and looked for something she could use as a weapon.

On top of the makeshift workbench was a rubber mallet. Effective for knocking wooden fence beams into place, but not the best option for self defense. Next to the mallet was a rusty handsaw, which might be good for spreading tetanus, but wouldn't do much in a fight. She grabbed the mallet and positioned herself next to the doorway. Whoever came through wouldn't see her until she got at least one swing off.

As the door opened slowly, Regan slipped to the back of the shack and tried to hide between several spare fenceposts. Ellie waited for someone to come in, her knuckles turning white around the mallet's wooden handle, but the only thing that entered was a tall shadow of a man in a cowboy hat cast upon on the dirt floor.

"Why don't you come on out of there?" said the man. "You're not in any trouble, but come out and let me have a look 'atcha."

The girls didn't answer. Finally, the man stepped inside. As he came in, Ellie steadied the mallet. When he turned and she saw him, she made a split-second decision not to pummel the old man. Knowing she couldn't stop the momentum of her swing, she released her grip on the handle, letting the mallet fall to the ground. It was all she could do to keep from bludgeoning him.

"There's two of you?" he said. "Why are you in Bill Tonn's toolshed?"

"Who are you?" asked Ellie.

"I'm Bill Tonn. Friends call me Lucky."

Lucky Bill Tonn looked to be in his seventies. His face and hands were as weathered as his shed. He wore black leather chaps, a neatly pressed light blue shirt, and a large black cowboy hat. He reminded Ellie of someone she'd seen on a rodeo poster years ago. A pickup man is what the poster called him.

"Came out here to see if this shed was still standing after all that wind last night. Didn't think I'd find you two here. Who are you anyway?"

"We escaped," said Regan, climbing to her feet.

"We were kidnapped," said Ellie. "Can you get us to the

police?"

"Kidnapped? From where?"

"The police," repeated Ellie. "Can you get us to the police?"

"Of course I can." He waved them out of shed. "Come on. I'll take you now."

The girls stepped out of the shed and into the bright sun. The heat beat down on them, but it didn't seem as hot as yesterday.

"Bill Tonn," said a woman. "What you got there?"

Ellie looked up to see a woman Bill's age standing next to a faded red pickup. It was an older model, the kind with the rounded hood and headlights that looked like eyeballs.

"These two girls need to go to the police. Say they were kidnapped."

"Kidnapped? Where from?"

Bill turned to the girls as if waiting for an answer.

"I was in a car accident in Big Rock. A man took me." Ellie pointed to Regan. "They took her from Michigan."

"Oh my. We better get them to town."

"That's what I was gonna do, woman."

Bill walked to the back of the truck, dropped the narrow lift gate, and helped the girls into the back.

"Are we near Big Rock?" asked Ellie.

"We're not near anything. But I can get you there in about an hour or so."

Ellie nodded. "Thank you."

Bill closed the lift gate and walked to the driver's door.

"And, Lucky," said Ellie. "Don't stop anywhere but the police station."

"Will do, little lady. You two just sit tight and I'll get you there safe and sound."

Regan had propped herself up against the back of the cab, but Ellie pulled her down so she was flat against the bed. "No one can see us," she said. "Anyone could be out here."

Lucky Bill Tonn started the truck and rolled away from the toolshed as Ellie and Regan held hands in the back.

There wasn't much to hang on to while lying flat in the back, so Ellie felt every bump as the road tossed her about. Twice, she thought she might bounce out of the truck, but both times she landed safely on her back, even if her head did ricochet off the metal bed a few times. She watched the sun in the sky directly above and figured that's what would have gotten them. The sun. Little John and an isolated prison couldn't break her, but Mother Nature could have punched her ticket. Lucky Bill Tonn saved her. Maybe she was the lucky one.

The trip passed quickly, and Ellie didn't raise her head until the truck stopped and the engine fell silent. When she sat up, she was staring at the front door to the Big Rock Police Department. For the first time in what felt like a week, a smile crossed her face.

"Told ya I'd get you here," said Bill. "Come on out of there."

Bill dropped the lift gate, helped Ellie and Regan out of the back, and escorted them into the building.

"Can I help you?" asked the man behind the desk.

"I'm Bill Tonn. I live a ways out. I found these two young'uns in my toolshed. They said they've been kidnapped. Asked me to bring them here."

"Kidnapped?" said the officer. "By who?"

"I don't know," said Ellie. "We were in a basement. There was another girl there too, but they took her somewhere else. We escaped."

"We may have killed a man," said Regan. "But we had to do it to get out."

The man stood up. "Okay, we'll get to all that. What's your names?"

"Ellie Armstrong."

"Regan Simmons."

"Okay, Ellie and Regan. We've been looking for you, Ellie. Your father was in an accident. He's in the hospital."

"Is he okay?"

"I don't know." He circled the girls. "Are you hurt? Injured or anything?"

"I might have a broken nose," said Ellie. "My head hurt a few days ago, but it's better now."

"How about you?"

"I'm okay," said Regan.

"Okay. Let's do this. I want to get you to the hospital. You both look severely dehydrated, and I want a doctor to look at you. I'll take your statements there and we'll get to the bottom of this." He turned to Bill. "And what did you say your name was?"

"Bill Tonn. Lucky Bill Tonn."

"Thank you for bringing them here, Bill."

"You're welcome. And what's your name?"

"Sergeant Willie Hatson."

25

THE FAT MAN AND THE SILVER FOX

"Do you know where they kept you?" asked Sergeant Hatson as he opened the rear door to one of the department's patrol cars. "Or who took you?"

"A woman took me," said Regan. "In Michigan."

"And you?"

"I don't remember. I was in the accident with my father. When I woke up, I was in a vehicle with a bag on my head. They took me into some underground room. Like a cistern or something. Regan and Jen were already there."

He helped them into the back, closed the door, then climbed into the front of the cruiser. "Jen? That's the girl who they moved somewhere else?"

"Right," said Ellie. "We don't know where. How does this all work? How are you going to find them?"

"One step at a time. First, I'm taking you both to the hospital to get checked out. I'll get all the details I can there. Regan, you can call your parents. I'm sure they're worried sick about you. After all that, I'll get a statement with all the details you can provide. And then we'll start looking for the bastards who did this. Right now, just try to rest. We'll be at the hospital in about a half hour." Hatson removed his cell phone, held it up, and snapped a photo of Ellie.

"What's that for?"

"Do you know a Connor Harding?"

"No."

"You've never heard of him?"

"No, why?"

"He's heard of you. Been looking for you for the past week."

"Why?"

"I don't know. But he's very persistent. Says he's a friend of your father's. I'm going to send him this photo and let him know you're all right."

Ellie watched as Hatson typed out a message and set the phone down. He fired the engine and pulled out of the lot.

Tim Waters's cell phone dinged. He looked at the familiar blue-haired girl in the photo and read the message. After stuffing the phone back into his pocket, he went to get his rifle.

Ellie closed her eyes and for the first time felt safe. The ever-present panic that had engulfed her for the past several days faded into the background. It was replaced with the optimism of seeing her father again, even if he was in a hospital bed. She thought about Regan and what she would do next. She had said she never knew her parents and had lived in foster care for years. Would she go back to Michigan? Back to the coffee shop where she worked?

She let her eyes close and drifted off to sleep. A pothole woke her. She bounced up and into the window. It reminded her of the ride in the bed of Lucky Bill Tonn's red pickup. It took her a moment to realize they were no longer on the main road.

Ellie knew these roads. There weren't many of them, but she knew where the hospital was in relation to the police station. She turned to Regan, who was also asleep, unaware of the pothole or the road deviation.

"Where are you going?" asked Ellie.

"To the hospital, like I said. To get you checked out."

"This isn't the way to the hospital."

"Relax," said Hatson. "Just go back to sleep and we'll be there in no time."

Was she wrong? Was this the way to the hospital? Perhaps the sergeant was taking an unfamiliar route.

Resting her heard against the glass, she peered out the window and watched the roadside flash by.

Connor was sitting in the lobby of the Frontier Inn contemplating his next move. He'd go back to the Pale Mare Ranch again, but this time he'd get a closer look at the place. No binoculars needed. His cell phone vibrated on the cracked wooden side table.

Looking for me?

Connor waited as an image downloaded. Slowly, line by line, a photo emerged. Ellie.

He snatched the phone from the table.

Who is this? he typed.

If you want to see the girl again, come to Rentschler Park. Alone. One hour.

Connor's first instinct was to call Officer Burton, but there was something about Burton he didn't trust. It seemed Burton had proven himself a competent lawman, but he was too close to the Hatsons, and Connor wasn't certain where his allegiance lie. The steel grille in the photo suggested the image of Ellie was taken in the back of a squad car. Burton wasn't off the hook yet.

Connor's cell phone slowed to a crawl as he searched for directions to Rentschler Park. Once he downloaded them, he went to his room. In the bathroom, he removed the toilet tank lid, reached into the cold water, and retrieved the watertight bag. He ripped it open, removed the black box, and opened it to get to his .45.

He racked the slide, ensuring he had a round in the chamber, and headed out the door.

When you live in a small town, you get to know the roads, and Ellie knew Big Rock well enough, at least the parts she frequented. She knew the hospital was north of town. It was near the pizza joint she and her father visited every Friday night. She had passed the Big Rock Hospital from nearly every direction, but never from this road.

"This isn't right," said Ellie. "This isn't the way to the hospital."

Regan was awake now too.

Hatson didn't answer. He didn't even try to lie.

Regan looked at Ellie, who shook her head.

"You're a cop," continued Ellie. "Where are you taking us?"

"You got pretty far, you know that?" said Hatson. "I figure you made it about fifteen miles. That's a long way, especially with no shoes."

"What are you doing?" asked Regan, kicking the back of the passenger seat.

"I'm taking you back where you belong."

"You son of a bitch!" Ellie's scream pierced the air. It was loud enough for Hatson to cover his ear with his free hand.

"You know you two really did a number on Sammy. Busted him up real bad. Put him in the hospital. Two broken legs and a fractured hip and wrist." Ellie caught his eyes in the rearview mirror. "You two are pretty tough for little things."

"Give me the chance and I'll show you how tough I am."

"Settle down, girlie. You can be as tough as you want here, but it won't matter. Whoever gets you on the receiving end, he'll break you. He'll break you real good."

"Where are you sending us?" said Regan, still kicking the seat.

"Don't know. Whoever's willing to pay for you."

Ellie turned to Regan. The finality hit her. Until know, this was a kidnapping. Ellie didn't know the end game. She had suspected it, but this was the first time it was crystal clear. They were being trafficked. They were being sold.

The cruiser pulled off the road, and a mile or so later stopped at a house. Ellie didn't recognize it. It had been dark when they escaped, and while she didn't get a good look at the house when they left, she was confident this wasn't the same place. But where were they?

Ellie started on the window, slamming her fist into it until she lost feeling in her hand. Hatson's words echoed in her head. "He'll break you real good." Rolling on her back, Ellie kicked violently at the window. She watched it bow under the repeated blows, but the glass didn't budge.

Regan joined in. She turned so she was back-to-back with Ellie and started kicking the other window. The glass didn't break. Of course it wouldn't. This was a police car. The windows were made to withstand physical onslaughts from passengers who wanted nothing more than to get out. What chance did they have?

As Hatson opened the door and walked away from the car, the girls turned their attention back to the steel divider between the front and rear seats. A mount on the dashboard secured a shotgun next to the steering wheel. Get through the grate to that and this was over. She'd make sure of that.

She began kicking the divider, and after a moment, Regan joined in. They pounded the grate with everything they had, determined to bust it out or break their legs trying. But it wasn't enough.

A moment later, Hatson returned to the car with two men Ellie had never seen before. One was as wide as a bus and looked like a farmhand. He had some sort of rod in his hand. The other was an older man with neatly combed gray hair and scruff on his face.

Hatson opened the door and Ellie was the first to get out. She wanted to bolt past the farmhand and never look back. She was calculating the best way past him when he jabbed the metal rod into her stomach. Blinding pain surged through her, radiating from her abdomen outward. Her body jerked and she fell to the ground shaking uncontrollably. The sensation passed a moment later, and she clawed at the ground, trying to get a grip on something to find her balance. Getting up on one knee, she felt like a sprinter waiting for the starting pistol to fire. The men stepped away from her, giving her space, and she saw a way through. Right between the fat man and the silver fox. They'd both be slow, and Hatson, he'd never catch her either. She was running for freedom and nothing would stand in her way. In her head, the starting pistol cracked and she jumped forward. The big man brought the rod down again. This time, he jabbed and jabbed. Three blinding shocks and she hit the ground. Another two shocks and her eyes went dark.

Somewhere behind her, Regan screamed.

26

MISSED OPPORTUNITIES

CONNOR FOLLOWED the gravel road off the highway for several miles before he found Rentschler Park. Despite its name, it wasn't a park at all. It was a mine, or at least what was left of one. He rolled toward two dilapidated buildings. The one with the faded red tin roof was leaning so far to one side it looked drunk. The other building, a three-story structure covered in vertical pine boards, had an open tower on one side with all sorts of cables and pulleys attached to it. On the opposite side, a track curved away from the building and descended down into the ground.

Positioned between two mountains, the site was in the middle of nowhere. It was a good place to disappear, which Connor knew was the reason he was there. He was getting close to finding Ellie, and whoever sent the photo wanted to end things before he got any closer.

He'd arrived fifteen minutes early, but knew whoever sent that text message was already here, waiting for him. He kept the truck moving, slightly swerving side to side in case someone was trying to scope him in through the windshield.

If someone was going to take a shot at him, it would likely come from one of the three window frames at the top of the taller building. The window panes were long gone, or perhaps there was never any glass there, but the openings' vantage point over the desolate landscape made him nervous. If Connor was orchestrating an ambush, that's where he'd set up. That position offered line of sight to the entire gravel road, and anyone up there would be able to see Connor coming from a mile away.

Connor rolled to a stop close enough to one of the building's entrances that he wouldn't be out in the open. After stopping the car, he grabbed the .45 and dashed inside. Moving carefully along the interior wall, he peered up to the top of the building. The inside was open, with various wooden beams and tracks that went in every direction. The place looked like Grand Central Station for mine cars. Sun came through the broken slats in the walls, casting a yellow glow across the ground. Connor continued along the wall. Two more steps and a crack echoed through the building as part of the pine wall in front of him exploded outward. He looked up for a moment before retreating through the same door he had entered. Whoever fired the shot was camped out above him somewhere on the tracks.

Outside, Connor moved around the building, where he found a rusty ladder bolted to the side. Keeping the .45 in his hand, he slowly climbed to the upper level being a quiet as possible. When he reached the top, he peered through the opening, hoping to get a glimpse of whoever fired the shot. Climbing through the opening and onto a mine car track, he heard rustling below him. Looking down, he spotted a large man carrying a rifle darting out through a side entrance.

Connor turned and went back down the ladder. When he reached the ground, he heard a diesel engine roaring.

A moment later, a black pickup truck rounded the leaning building and barreled toward him leaving a wake of dust behind it. The ground vibrated as Connor raised the .45 and waited for his shot. The sun reflected off the chrome grille creating bursts of blinding light. When it was close enough for Connor see the driver through the windshield, he lined up his shot and fired, emptying the magazine. The vehicle was some fifty feet away before it veered slightly to the right and crashed through the pine building.

Connor backed away from the building, half expecting it to come crashing down on top of the truck. He waited but the structure held. Satisfied the building wouldn't collapse, Connor slowly crept toward the truck, which had slammed into a vertical beam thick enough to withstand the force of a locomotive. He opened the driver's door and found a man with his face buried in a white airbag. He turned off the still-running engine, disengaged the seatbelt, and dragged the man out of the cab and onto the ground.

Four of Connor's shots had hit him. Not bad for firing into a moving vehicle. Connor grabbed the man's thick arm just above an anchor tattoo, and his waistband, and rolled him onto his chest. Searching the man's rear pocket, Connor found his wallet and pulled out the driver's license. The dead man still bleeding in front of him was Tim Waters.

"That's enough," said McMurphy, waving the farmhand off. He turned to the girls. "You two got pretty far," he said.

"Not far enough," said Ellie, staggering to her knees.

"Give yourself some credit. I've been doing this for a long time, and you're the first to ever escape. Well, I guess you didn't really escape because here you are, but you did give me a bit of a scare. The last thing I need is the two of you running across Wyoming." McMurphy turned to Hatson. "Who else knows about this?"

"Some rancher named Bill Tonn. He and his wife picked them up and brought them in."

"I know Bill," said McMurphy. "Good guy. Sorry these two brought him into this. His ranch is about twelve miles northwest of here. Go take care of him. His old lady too."

"Leave him alone," said Ellie, getting to her feet. "He was only trying to help us."

"I know, and now you've got him killed. See, your actions have consequences. That man you nearly killed in the basement? He's in the hospital. Likely never walk right again. He's having a hellava time talking too. I didn't know you had it in you."

"Maybe if you weren't kidnapping women none of this would have happened," said Regan from the back seat of the cruiser.

"Maybe," said McMurphy. "But that's neither here nor there. Now I have to figure out what to do with you two." Murphy turned to the farmhand. "Call Jeremiah and tell him I need a transfer. He can get the redhead first."

"No!" said Ellie.

"Don't worry, firecracker. You'll be right behind her. You're going in a different direction though, gotta split you up." He started back to his truck. "Bring 'em over."

The fat man grabbed Ellie from behind, wrapping his arms around her and lifting her off the ground in a bear hug.

Hatson pulled Regan out of the back of the cruiser, pinned her arms behind her and walked her to McMurphy's pickup.

"Don't hurt 'em now," said Hatson, unzipping a case in the back seat.

He pulled out a glass vile, stabbed a syringe into it, and drew back the plunger.

"You first, firecracker," he said.

"Stop!" said Ellie, kicking.

McMurphy dodged her legs as they flailed in every direction.

"Hey, you speak Spanish?" asked McMurphy.

"No," said Ellie, still kicking.

"That's too bad. You're going to have a rough go where you're headed."

McMurphy jabbed her in the shoulder and pressed the plunger down. He removed the syringe, careful not to snap the needle off as she tried to kick him. She'd stopped struggling before McMurphy could cap the needle and collapsed into the big man's arms.

"She won't be any more trouble," said McMurphy. "Take her to the cottage. I'll take the other one to the ranch." He turned to Regan. "You're next, red."

Hatson pushed Regan against the pickup truck and put his forearm across her neck.

McMurphy prepped another syringe, then grabbed Regan's leg with his free hand and jabbed her thigh. He pressed the plunger down, slipped it out of her leg, and watched as her eyes rolled back and her body relaxed.

27

A RECKONING

THE PHONE RANG on Chief Hatson's desk. He nearly knocked his coffee over trying to answer it, but caught the teetering cup before it soaked his desktop. .

"Chief Hatson."

"Hello." The woman on the other end of the line paused, as if not knowing what to say. "Is this the Big Rock Police Department?"

"Yes. Is there something I can do for you, ma'am?"

"I was calling about those two girls. Or young ladies, I suppose. My name is Martha Tonn. My husband, Bill, brought those girls in yesterday. I wanted to see if they were okay."

Chief Hatson slid the coffee cup aside and rested his elbows on the desk.

"Martha, say that again please?"

"I wanted to see if those girls were all right. We found them in our toolshed yesterday. They said they'd been kidnapped. I hope they're okay now."

"How old were these girls?"

"Not too young. Teenagers, I guess. Strange hair. One was red and the other blue. Bright blue. Reminded me of a peacock."

Chief Hatson raised his eyes to find Officer Burton reading a book at his desk. He glanced back down at his phone and twirled his index finger, wrapping the phone cord around it.

"You're telling me you found two girls in your toolshed and you brought them here? Yesterday?"

"That's right. My husband and I. He said he was going to take them to the hospital."

"Who said that?"

"The officer. I don't know his name. I didn't come inside. Just Bill did. He said not to call you because you've got important things going on, but I just had to. Those girls didn't look good."

"What time did your husband come in yesterday?"

"Around suppertime."

Chief Hatson scribbled down Martha's number from the screen. "Ma'am, I'm sorry to say I wasn't here yesterday, and this is the first I'm hearing about all this. But I promise you, I'll look into it. You can bet on that."

Chief Hatson hung up and dialed the hospital. A moment later, he confirmed what he feared. After hanging up with the hospital, he double-timed it to Burton's desk.

"You here yesterday?"

"Until just after lunch. Then I was on patrol in town until about six before heading home. Why?"

"Where was my son while you were on patrol?"

"Here, I suppose."

Chief Hatson looked back toward his office. He swayed a

bit and had to grab the corner of Burton's desk for support.

"You okay, Chief? Something wrong?"

"No. Fine. I've gotta go follow up on something. Cover the phones?"

"Of course. Shout if you need help with anything."

"Will do."

Chief Hatson went for the door, but stopped at the corkboard next to the window. He ripped down the piece of paper with Connor's phone number and stuffed it in his pocket.

When Chief Hatson arrived at the home on Buffalo Trace, the driveway was empty. He clicked on his police radio.

"Sergeant Hatson, you copy?"

"Copy. What's going on, Pop?"

"Where are you?"

"Headed over to Bill Tonn's ranch. He called and said some of his cattle were missing. Wanted me to come out and have a look."

"Bill Tonn, you say?"

"That's right."

"Why don't you meet me at your house first. I need to talk to you in person. It's important."

"Can it wait until I see Bill? He seemed really adamant about me coming out there."

"Bill Tonn can wait. Meet me at your place ASAP." He thought for a moment. "It's about Connor Harding. See you soon."

Chief Hatson clicked off his radio, turned off his car, and waited.

· · ·

Sergeant Willie Hatson arrived twenty minutes later. He stepped out of his car to find his father sitting on the hood of his cruiser.

"What's going on, Pops?"

"What in the fuck have you gone and gotten yourself into, son?"

"What are you talking about?"

"Got a call at the station. Wanted to follow up on the two girls they dropped off. The red- and blue-haired ones."

"Pop, I don't—"

"Cut the shit, son. Where are they now?"

Willie was quiet.

"What are you wrapped up in?"

"It's McMurphy. They're with him."

"That's the Ellie girl that Harding fella is looking for. You've been throwing him off the scent since he got here. How long have you known about her?"

"I just found out about her. Look, it's not what you think. McMurphy called me and said one of his ranch hands brought these girls back from The Hunting Lodge the other night to have a little fun. Said he's got a no girls policy, and as soon as he found them at the bunkhouse, he told one of his boys to take them home. As far as McMurphy knew, that's what happened. Then this Bill Tonn shows up with the girls saying they were kidnapped and what have you."

"Where are the girls now?"

"I took them back to the ranch to get everyone's stories. The whole kidnapping thing was bullshit. You know how girls are. They were mad McMurphy kicked them out of the bunkhouse. That's all."

"You left them with McMurphy?"

"He said he was going to get to the bottom of it. Find out why the ranch hand didn't take them home like he said. He gave me his word he'd make sure they get home safe and sound."

Chief Hatson slid off the hood of his car.

"Get in," he said.

"What?"

"Get in the car. We're going to see McMurphy and talk this through. If that girl's a minor, like Harding said she was, then McMurphy's got some explaining to do. And what about this other girl? I'm sure her parents are worried sick. Jesus Christ."

"Pop, we—"

"And if they're still at the ranch, then I'll remove them myself."

"All right." Willie nodded and followed his father toward his cruiser.

"You must have cow shit between your ears. That badge you got there, it means something. It ain't just for show. You've got a job to protect the people of Big Rock, young girls and all. And if you can't do that, then as far as I'm concerned, you don't deserve to wear it. You just better pray those girls are okay when we get there."

Chief Hatson reached into his pocket and pulled out the piece of paper. "Suppose we should call Harding too. Tell him we found his girl before he tears up the rest of the town looking for her."

The chief opened the car door. He had one leg in the cruiser when Willie fired his service revolver.

28

TWO DEAD MEN AND A REDHEAD

IF TIM WATERS was involved in Ellie's disappearance, then McMurphy was too. Connor needed hard evidence to move on McMurphy, and sending his henchmen to kill him checked the box.

Connor returned to his rental and headed back to the Pale Mare Ranch. An hour later, he was perched atop the same hill he and Burton had used earlier. He lay down in the dirt and peered through Ginny's binoculars.

For the first two hours, the only thing he saw was a bison rubbing against a fencepost to shed its molting coat. After repositioning himself to escape a leg cramp, Connor peeked through the binoculars again. This time something else caught his attention. A box truck was barreling down the dirt road that served as McMurphy's driveway. After the truck stopped in front of the main home, two men stepped out of the cab and raised the rear door. A moment later, a big man in overalls came out carrying a woman with red hair. They both went into the back of the truck, but only the big guy came out. As soon as his feet hit the ground, the two men closed the rear door, returned to the cab and pulled away. Before the truck reached the end of the driveway, Connor was running toward his truck parked a quarter mile away.

Inside his rental, Connor fired the engine and hit the gas. There was only one road out to the McMurphy Ranch, and he knew if he put the accelerator to the floor, he'd catch the truck before it got too far. It only took a few minutes before he saw it through his windshield. Another minute and he was riding the truck's back bumper. He passed the truck, pulled ahead, and put some distance between the two vehicles. Since he was in front, there was no chance he was going to lose them on the two-lane road. He pulled further ahead and watched the truck shrink in his rearview mirror.

There was an unconscious woman in the back of the box truck, and as far as Connor was concerned there was no legitimate reason for her to be there. Ellie might be there too, which meant searching the truck. First, he had to stop it.

About a mile up the road, he stopped, did a two-point turn, and parked diagonally across the road. He hit the hazards for emphasis. He hoped the truck would stop, but if they decided to go around Connor, they would have to pull off onto the shoulder, slowing them down. That might be all Connor needed to get a shot off.

Slipping out of the rental, he stood behind it, concealing his reloaded .45 in one hand and frantically waiving the other. He'd given himself enough room to maneuver out of the way if the truck decided to ram him, but he suspected that was a last resort. Whoever was in the cab had no idea who Connor was and likely wouldn't risk ripping their own vehicle apart trying to drive through a parked car, especially with precious cargo in the back. It was a gamble Connor was willing to take.

And it paid off.

The oncoming truck slowed and stopped about twenty feet from Connor's pickup. The passenger, a thin man in a hooded sweatshirt, stepped down from the cab and walked toward Connor carrying a baseball bat. It was a bad decision on his part. Connor fired twice, dropping him. The driver kicked the truck into reverse and rolled backward, trying to get enough clearance to get around Connor's truck. Raising the weapon, Connor dialed in the target. He waited for the truck to stop, but it surged forward in a puff of diesel smoke. He fired three times through the windshield and the truck veered off the road and rolled to a stop as the driver slumped over to the side.

Connor opened the door and killed the engine. Yanking the keys from the ignition, he carried them to the back of the truck. The smaller of the two keys opened the padlock on the rear door. After removing that, he raised the back door and stepped to the side, out of view from anyone who might be ready to return fire from inside the back.

He raised his weapon and peered around the side to find the redhead unconscious on a mattress that took up half the cargo area. He climbed inside and noticed sweat and blood stains covered the mattress. They'd used it before. Lots of times.

Connor checked the girl's pulse. It was faint, but it was there. He tucked the .45 in his waistband, carried her back to his truck, and laid her down in the back seat. One at a time, he scooped the two dead men off the hot pavement and hoisted them into the back of the box truck. Then he closed the door and left the truck beside the road. Maybe someone would stop to investigate. Maybe not.

When he returned to the rental, he tossed his weapon into the glove box and pointed the truck toward Big Rock.

29

ITCHY FINGERS

Officer Burton was searching the Internet for anything he could find on Ken McMurphy. From everything he knew about the rancher, he was a stand-up guy, pillar of the community type. He was a successful businessman, but had he built that success by wrangling horses or something else?

He was knee-deep in the digital archives of the *Casper Star-Tribune* when Sergeant Hatson kicked the front door open and ran into the police department.

"Get in the cruiser now!"

Burton shot up from his desk and clicked the browser closed. "What?"

"We're bringing in Connor Harding."

"Bringing him in? On what charge?"

"Murder."

"Murder? What are you talking about?"

"Connor Harding killed my father. Shot him in the back like a coward."

"Slow down, Sergeant. He shot your father?"

"Shot him twice in the back. He was still alive when I found him." Hatson moved erratically, as if powered by cigarettes and energy drinks. "He said Harding followed him to my home and was asking questions about Ken McMurphy. He's got it in his head that Ken has something to do with this missing girl. He's crazy. My father tried to get him to calm down and Harding shot him."

"He told you all this after he was shot?"

"That's right."

"Where's your father now?"

"Still at my house. He died in my arms, Kyle. And Harding is going to pay for it. Let's go." Hatson moved like a hummingbird. He darted into his father's office and returned with a shotgun.

"Sergeant, this doesn't make any sense. Why would he shoot your father?"

Hatson racked the shotgun. "Damnit, Kyle. I'm bringing Harding in even if I have to go through you to do it."

It didn't make any sense to Burton, but Hatson was in no frame of mind to be rational. Maybe, given some time to calm down, Burton could get more information from him. Burton wasn't an expert on Connor Harding, and while he'd seen the fire in his eyes at Tim Waters's home, he didn't seem likely to murder the chief of police in cold blood.

"Where are we going?" he asked.

"He's staying at the Frontier Inn. I think Ginny is protecting him for some reason. She said he wasn't there, but he's in room five. Follow me there!"

Hatson charged out of the building as Burton fumbled with his keys.

· · ·

Hatson was the first one out of the cruiser when they arrived at the Frontier Inn. He exploded through the lobby doors like a stick of dynamite.

"Where the fuck is he, Ginny?"

By the time Burton made it into the lobby, Hatson was dragging Ginny out of her office by her hair.

"Sergeant!"

Hatson turned and raised the shotgun at Burton. "Stay the fuck back or I'll put you through that wall!"

Burton raised his hands. "Sergeant, you need to calm down and—"

"Don't you tell me to calm down. That sonofabitch murdered my father and I'm bringing him in." He turned the shotgun back to Ginny. "Where is he? I know he's staying here!"

Ginny covered her head and cowered on the floor in front of the counter. "He's not here. I haven't seen him."

Hatson grabbed her by the shirt, pulled her off the floor, and pushed her against the counter.

"Sergeant!"

"She's harboring a murderer and I intend to find him."

Burton moved between Ginny and Hatson and eased the sergeant back. "Ginny, if you know where Harding is, we need you to tell us."

"I don't know where he is. He's staying in room five, but I don't know where he is now. I haven't seen him today. I just don't know."

"Sergeant, give me the shotgun and I'll go check out his room. Maybe there's something in there that can tell us where he went."

Hatson stared at Burton and lowered the shotgun. Maybe he was acting a bit unhinged. Maybe Ginny needed a softer approach.

"Okay," said Hatson, handing Burton the shotgun. "Check out his room."

Burton took the weapon and looked at Ginny for a few long moments before taking the master key from the key rack and leaving the lobby for Harding's room.

"You've been lying to me, Ginny. When I came in earlier, you said Harding wasn't staying here. Are you aiding and abetting a fugitive?"

"I don't know anything about a fugitive. He said he was looking for a missing girl, that's all I know. I swear. He comes and goes. He doesn't stop in to tell me where he's going."

"Why should I believe you?"

"Because I'm telling you the truth."

"I don't think you are." Hatson drew his service revolver. "Harding doesn't have anyone else in town. He doesn't know anyone here except you."

"How would I even be able to help him? I don't know anything about a missing girl."

"Do you have a way to contact him?"

"No. He didn't leave a phone number. I'm just renting him the room."

Hatson swiped the ledger from the counter and threw it at her. "He's not in the ledger. I checked the last time I was here."

"He didn't want to be in there."

"So you are helping him. You're protecting him!"

"No. He said he wanted the room off the books. That's all. Please, put the gun away."

"How do I know you won't warn him when we're gone?"

"I told you, I have no way to reach him. I don't have his phone number."

"But when he comes back, how do I know you won't tell him we're looking for him?"

Her eyes were on the revolver. "I'm not going to tell him anything. I promise. You can stay here and wait for him."

"I don't have time to wait for him." He raised the revolver and brought it down on her.

Burton opened the door to room five and stepped inside. Harding wasn't in, but it was obvious someone was staying in the room. A closed suitcase sat on the middle of the king-sized bed and next to that was a smaller, black plastic box. Burton set the shotgun on the mattress and opened the suitcase to find some clothes, a handful of granola bars, and a half empty bottle of eye drops.

He turned his attention to the black box next to the suitcase. He opened it and ran his fingers across the dark-gray foam lining. The only thing inside was an open padlock.

Burton reached into his pocket for his cell phone and dialed. After four rings, the call went to voicemail.

"Shit, Harding, what in the hell is going on? Sergeant Hatson says you killed his father. That can't be right. He's on a tear looking for you. I've been looking into McMurphy, but I didn't find anything to connect him to any missing girls. I don't know if you've found anything. Call me when you get this, and stay away from—" Burton heard the floor creak.

When he turned around, Hatson was standing in front of him.

30

THE MAN IN ROOM TWENTY-THREE

As soon as Connor walked into the emergency room lobby at the Hale Medical Center, two nurses swarmed him. The sight of someone carrying an unconscious woman tends to set off alarm bells. Working together, the nurses took her from his arms and eased her into a wheelchair. One of the nurses whisked her away while the other hurled questions at Connor like a major league pitcher.

He replied to the onslaught of questions with, "I found her this way," "I think she's been drugged," and "I don't know." He said he found her on the roadside, which was technically correct, but he left out the details about the two dead men and the box truck.

The nurse told him to take a seat, but after she disappeared through two swinging doors, Connor left the waiting area for the third floor. He hadn't made if far off the elevator before he heard a familiar voice.

"I've been trying to reach you." Erin Duke pushed a med cart toward him.

"Why's that?"

"See for yourself." She parked the cart and headed down the hallway. Connor followed. She led him to a room where Aiden Armstrong sat up in bed eating a small cup of Jell-O.

"He's been awake and alert for two days. I tried reaching you but couldn't get through. Must be the bad phone service."

"How is he?"

"Seems pretty good. He's been asking about his daughter. He used the room phone to call the police but said he hasn't gotten any answers yet."

Connor looked at the man in the pale blue hospital gown and socks. Aiden would have no idea what had been happening since his accident, and Connor wasn't sure what to tell him. He didn't have many answers himself.

Aiden looked at Connor and adjusted his cracked glasses. "Do I know you?"

Erin walked Connor inside the room, where he sat down in an empty chair.

"No, you don't. I'm Connor Harding."

"So, you're the one my sister talked about? You look like a bull rider."

"I'm too old for that."

"Zoe said she sent you to find my daughter."

"What else did she tell you?"

"She told me to stop trying the police. That they weren't going to help. Is that right?"

"That's right."

"Did you find her?"

"Not yet. But I will."

"You realize how hard it is to sit here and wait for some news? It's killing me. She's my daughter, and she's all I've got." He shifted in the bed. "I want to do something, but I don't know what."

"You're good right where you are," said Connor. "It's the best place for you right now."

"You went to my home?"

"There's no sign of her there."

Connor went on to explain everything Zoe had told him. About how the hospital reached out to her, and she to him. He didn't mention the favor he owed her.

"Then where is she?"

Connor wished he had more answers to give him. He felt like a failure, as if he had been responsible for Ellie all along or that he should have been able to find her by now. He had found dangerous enemy combatants in less time.

"What do you remember about the accident?" asked Connor.

Aiden thought for a moment and rubbed his head. "I remember coming back from getting pizza with Ellie. There was an accident, then I woke up here. That's about it. Did you call the police about Ellie?"

"Yes, but they've been no help. Zoe said you worked with the FBI. Were you investigating anyone in Big Rock?"

"Investigating? Hell no. I'm a consultant, I don't investigate anyone. I do research for the bureau. Go to Washington a few times a year to deliver reports to the higher-ups. I'm not in the field. Why?"

"Shit. I think someone has your daughter, and I thought maybe it was related to your work."

"Who would have her?"

"I think Ken McMurphy is involved. Ever hear of him?"

"The horse guy? Why would he have Ellie?"

"I don't know, but I just brought in a young woman about Ellie's age. I found her near McMurphy's ranch. I'm hoping she can help."

"We need to go to the police," said Aiden. "You need to tell them about McMurphy and this girl. It's been too long. Something is very wrong."

"Like I said, I tried that. It didn't work, so I'm doing it my way. I find that to be more effective anyway."

"Then I figure that's why my sister sent you. I don't agree with Zoe in most regards, but I assume if you're tied in with her then you know what you're doing. But listen, Connor. Ellie's all I got. You have to find her."

Erin poked her head into the room. "The girl you brought in, she's awake."

"I need to talk to her." He turned to Aiden. "I'll do everything I can to find Ellie. You've got my word."

Erin led Connor through a back corridor, which led to a stairwell to the emergency room area.

"She's got to be in one of these rooms," said Erin. "We've got a small ER wing."

The redhead was in the second room they checked. When Connor entered, the girl recoiled back on the bed, scrunching herself against the wall.

"Sir!" said a nurse who looked large enough to give Connor a run for his money. "Get out of this room!"

Erin stepped in. "Dawn, he's the one who brought her in. He's looking for a missing girl, and she might have seen her. He's with the FBI."

"The FBI?" said Dawn, crossing her arms. "And you're going to show me a badge if I ask for one?"

"No," said Connor. "I'm going to give you some lame excuse why I don't have it."

"Dawn, please," said Erin.

"You got five minutes, but I'm not leaving this room."

"Thank you." Connor crouched by the side of the bed. "I'm Connor Harding and I'm looking for someone named Ellie Armstrong. She's seventeen and has blue hair." He reached into his pocket for his cell phone to show her the photo.

"I. I. Know her." Her words were slow and labored. "I can't think straight. Dizzy."

"She's been drugged," said Dawn. "I ran a tox screen, but we're not going to know what it is for a while."

"It's okay," said Connor, slowing down his words. "Can you tell me where Ellie is? I need to find her."

"We escaped."

"From where? McMurphy's ranch? Is Ellie with McMurphy?"

She nodded, but then shook her head. "No. Not the ranch."

"She's not at the ranch? She's somewhere else?"

She nodded.

"She's alive?"

She nodded again.

Connor took her hand between his. "I know it's hard to think right now, but I don't have a lot of time. Can you tell me where Ellie is now?"

"We escaped."

"I know you did. You escaped. I found you in a truck and brought you here. But Ellie wasn't in the truck." His felt his pace starting to quicken and slowed his words again. "Ellie was not with you. Do you know where she is?"

She shook her head.

"Shit."

"Sir, she needs to rest," said Dawn, approaching the bed. "It'll clear her head. Give her some time and she'll probably be able to help more."

"Cottage," said the girl.

"She's at a cottage?"

"Sir, please. She needs to rest."

There was no time. McMurphy would find out about the redhead, and if he did have Ellie, he'd move her. He'd know the walls were closing in and he'd have to do something.

Connor stood up, but the girl reached for his hand.

"We escaped. We hurt a man. Real bad."

"You hurt someone?" asked Connor.

She nodded. "Hospital."

Connor thought for a moment. "Wait, you hurt someone. Did they bring him to the hospital?"

She nodded.

"We're the only hospital around," said Erin. "If they brought him to a hospital, he's here."

Connor felt the girl's hand relax. When he turned back to the bed, she was asleep.

"You've got to go," said Dawn, pushing Connor out of the room. "If you want to wait in the lobby, I'll let you know when she wakes up again. Maybe she can be more help then."

Connor thanked her and left the room with Erin. She pulled him into a side hallway.

"Legally, I can't be telling you this," said Erin. "But they brought someone in the other day who had some serious injuries. The guy who dropped him off said it was in a bull riding accident. No way. I've treated plenty of those. This guy has bruises on his neck and two busted legs. Someone strangled him and beat him with something."

"Strangled?"

"Right. But he's not talking."

"Strangled and had his legs beaten? Seems like a two-man job. Or a two-woman job."

"I saw him yesterday. Second floor. Room twenty-three."

Connor thanked her and headed down the hall.

"Make sure he's the right guy," Erin called after him.

"He's the right guy."

The man in room twenty-three was awake when Connor walked into the room and closed the door behind him. Connor clicked on the overhead light and sat on the bed.

The man watched him remove his cell phone and hold up a photo.

"Do you recognize this girl?"

The man's eyes grew wide and he began to shake.

"I'll take that as a yes." Connor looked the man over. "Looks like those girls messed you up pretty bad." He leaned in next to his ear. "I'm going to finish the job."

The man tried to speak but only a whisper escaped.

"What?" said Connor. "Can't hear you."

There was a red ligature bruise about an inch wide around the man's neck. Connor wrapped a big hand around the man's throat and squeezed. He felt the man's neck muscles tense and watched as two veins bulged on opposite sides of his mouth. Connor let up and the color rushed back into his face.

"I'm going to choke you to death," said Connor. "And the only way you're going to survive this is if you tell me where they're keeping Ellie."

The man nodded and said something, but it was too faint for Connor to make out. "Again," he said, placing his ear next to the man's mouth.

"The cottage."

The words were faint, but this time, Connor understood. The girl had been right.

"Do you know where that is?"

The man nodded.

"Tell me."

The man labored to spit out the details. Connor took in every word.

31

A TRAIL OF BODIES

CONNOR FOLLOWED the man's directions, which took him past the Frontier Inn. As he passed, he saw a cruiser in the parking lot, its lights flashing red and blue bursts. He recognized it as Burton's cruiser from the number on the roof.

Connor didn't plan on telling Burton about McMurphy's cottage because he didn't need a tail. He'd tell Burton about the red-haired girl and send him to the hospital to get a statement.

As he pulled up to the cruiser, he saw Burton in the driver's seat, but when he stopped next to the vehicle, he realized something was wrong. Burton's head was cocked to the side in the kind of way that suggested a broken neck. Connor crouched and peered through the driver's window. There was a bullet hole on the left side of Burton's head, and a bigger mess on the passenger seat.

Connor grabbed his .45 from the rental's glove box and checked the parking lot. Besides Ginny's Taurus, the cruiser, and Connor's truck, the lot was empty.

Ginny!

Connor ran to the lobby door and peered inside, his weapon raised. Opening the door fully, he carefully moved through the lobby to the office. He found Ginny slouched over the desk, her head split open. He checked her pulse to confirm what he already suspected. When he glanced down, he saw a blood trail on the brown carpet. It was difficult to see, but it was there. Someone struck her in the lobby and then dragged her in here.

After checking the rest of the lobby, Connor went to his room, anticipating the shooter might be there, staking him out. Outside his room, he found the red curtain closed, something he always left open when he left. He gripped the .45 with both hands and drove his boot into the door just left of the knob. It flew open and bounced off the wall inside the room. Connor stopped it with his foot before it snapped closed again. He slowly moved inside, weapon raised, checking the room. The overturned suitcase told him someone had been there, but they were gone now.

"Hatson," said Connor.

He slipped his wallet from his back pocket and rifled through until he found what he was looking for, a business card with an embossed FBI logo and the contact information for Special Agent John Simmons.

He sat on the edge of the bed and dialed his cell phone, hoping the call would go through. After three attempts, it did. Agent Simmons didn't answer, but his voicemail did.

Connor left a detailed message, stuffed the phone in his pocket, and went back to his rental. He tore out of the parking lot with the steering wheel in one hand and the .45 in the other.

32

POKING THE BEAR

WHEN THE RED-HAIRED girl called it a cottage, Connor envisioned a small, quaint stone home covered in ivy, like something you would find in a fairytale book. McMurphy's place didn't fit that mold. It was more of a log cabin, but a modern take with square, hand-cut timbers and railings made from antlers. Next to the main house stood a stable with two ornate oak doors. Connor didn't know if it was a real barn or a garage designed to look like one.

McMurphy's black pickup was parked next to the house. It was the only car there. Connor was hoping to find Hatson's truck here too, two birds and all, but he'd deal with Hatson later.

He watched the house through Ginny's binoculars and was surprised McMurphy didn't have more manpower. He had hoped McMurphy didn't bring his ranch hands to the cottage. That would have made for a bigger mess. Did McMurphy know he was coming? He likely sent Tim Waters after him, and in his current state, Tim would not have checked in. McMurphy, if he was smart, would have feared the worst. One would think he would be on high alert. But Connor figured if there was a welcoming party it would be at the ranch. After all, McMurphy would have no way to know that Connor knew about the cottage. Maybe Hatson was waiting for him at the ranch too. He'd find out soon enough, but he had work to do here first.

There were a few interior lights on now, and Connor tracked three men moving through the house but saw no signs of Ellie. Glancing up at the roofline, Connor scanned the length of the house looking for floodlights or motion sensors but he didn't see any.

He wanted to charge the house, smash down the door, and lay waste to the place, but he had to be smart about it. He had to know what he was rushing into. He moved to the front of the house and peered around a large shrub and through the dining room window. Someone sat in a chair in the hall, but from his current angle, Connor couldn't see much else. He moved to another window, being sure to keep his head low. That window revealed more. In the hallway, a man in overalls sat with a shotgun across his lap. Next to him on the floor was a pack of smokes.

Given where the man sat, Connor was going to have a hard time getting to him. This wasn't some military operation where he could toss a flash-bang through the window, blow out the big man's eardrums and then take him out during the ensuing panic. Assuming they were locked, he'd have to break a window, giving away his position. And the last thing he wanted was to be on the business end of that shotgun. To hit something with a .45, you need to be accurate. But even in the hands of a novice, shotguns were bad news. You only had to aim in the general direction and the scatter would take care of the rest. Connor decided the safest move was to wait.

Thanks to the cigarettes, he didn't have to wait long. About a half hour later, the big man stood up, set the shotgun across the chair, and picked up the smokes. As he walked toward the back door, Connor shadowed him on the outside of the house, moving to the backyard. He waited at the corner until he heard the back door open. The next sound he heard was the flicking of a lighter.

Connor moved on him and had the .45 to his temple before the big man found a solid flame. He dropped the lighter on the ground and slowly turned his head to Connor, the unlit cigarette still dangling from his lips.

"The blue-haired girl, where is she?"

The big man hesitated.

Connor pushed the weapon against his head, nudging him backward. He didn't want to fire it. A .45 blasting off in the night would alert everyone else on the property that he was there, and he wanted to avoid that.

"One more time," said Connor. "Where is the girl?"

"The stable."

"Let's go."

Connor stepped aside and followed the man as he led him around the side of the house to the stable. He slipped a key into a locked side door and opened it. Connor followed him in. Ellie was slumped unconscious in the first stall, her hands shackled to the wall. Connor squinted and watched as her chest slowly rose and fell.

"What did you do to her?"

"Horse tranqs."

"The keys?"

The man pointed to a key ring hanging next to an electric cattle prod near the stable door.

"Who else is in the house?" asked Connor.

"Snider and McMurphy."

"And Hatson?"

The man shook his head.

"Okay." Connor brought the .45 down hard onto the man's temple and he dropped like an anchor. A lighter touch, and the man might take a long nap. But Connor hit him hard. Real hard. He wouldn't wake up.

Connor knelt and looked at Ellie, locked up like an animal. He thought about carrying her through the same hospital doors to the awaiting army of nurses. He wanted to see Aiden's face when he learned his daughter was safe and they were finally together again. He'd be happy to know this nightmare was over. But it wasn't over. Not yet.

Connor took the keys and unlocked Ellie's hands. After stashing the .45 in his belt, he picked up Ellie and carried her to the door of the stable. Before crossing the front yard, Connor watched the house for a moment. Satisfied no one was watching, he carried Ellie across the lawn and through the trees to his truck and laid her in the back seat.

"Sit tight, kiddo. I'll be back for you soon."

He gently closed the door and retraced his steps to the stable, where he grabbed the cattle prod.

Connor entered the house through the back door and moved to the stairs. He stopped every few steps and listened for McMurphy or anyone else who may be waiting for him. When he reached the top of the steps, he almost felt the silence. There wasn't another house around for miles, and except the stray call of a coyote, the night was still.

He peeked his head around the corner. The shot came almost instantly, but he recoiled fast enough that it missed him. Someone, Connor assumed it was Snider, was at the end for the hallway. Connor leapt down the stairs, dropping the cattle prod, as the man came around the corner and fired three more shots that tore through the light blue drywall. Connor ducked around the corner into the kitchen. He opened the steel refrigerator door, knelt behind it for cover, and waited. The man blindly fired three more shots into the kitchen as he made the turn. Two of his shots struck high on the refrigerator door. Connor steadied his hand and fired twice, putting both shots through the man's upper chest. He dropped, bouncing off the kitchen island, and slumped to the floor.

"That's two."

Connor went back to the stairs, retrieved the cattle prod from where he dropped it, and carefully made his way up to the second level. The man in the hallway was protecting someone, and it was likely McMurphy.

The first bedroom Connor came to was empty. The door to the next room was closed, but he could see light underneath the door.

"McMurphy, your men are dead." He tapped the cattle prod on the hallway wall. "Just like you're about to be."

The blast tore the bedroom door in half. Had Connor been standing in front of it, it would have been the last sound he heard.

He peeked his head around what was left of the doorframe to find McMurphy leveling a double-barrel shotgun at him. Connor darted out of the way as McMurphy fired the second blast into the hallway wall.

When Connor peered back into the room, he saw McMurphy struggling to push a cartridge into the shotgun's breech. Connor bolted into the room and jabbed the cattle prod into McMurphy's sternum. He screamed, dropped the shotgun, and fell backward onto the floor.

As Connor stood over him, the cattle prod grew heavier in his hand. He wanted to beat McMurphy with it and then shove it down his throat, or maybe see if the prongs would pierce through skin. Apply enough force and Connor could likely impale him. Decisions, decisions.

He kicked McMurphy in the ribs. "Get up!"

McMurphy writhed on the floor. He reached out for the shotgun, but Connor kicked it away.

"I said get up!"

The effects of the shock subsided and McMurphy found enough strength to get to his elbows and then to his feet.

"You had to know this was coming," said Connor. "I half expected a small army would be waiting for me."

"Are you here to kill me?"

"The thought crossed my mind."

"You seem like a reasonable man," said McMurphy, collecting his eyeglasses from the floor. "What can I do to change that?"

What else could McMurphy say? Everyone wants to bargain with the executioner, but was there anything that would truly save his life? Not likely, but he was willing to give it a go.

"Tell me why you did it."

"Why I did it?"

"Yeah. You seem to have a successful horse ranch. Why not stick to that?"

McMurphy was quiet and Connor wondered if McMurphy even knew why he did it.

"I got to dealing with the kind of people who get whatever they want. It just sort of happened."

"What kind of people?"

"The kind who want things others can't buy."

"Like girls," added Connor. "That's a sick type of individual."

"Some of these girls make out like bandits," said McMurphy. "They get a good life. Some of them even get a husband out of the deal."

Connor slipped the .45 into his waistband and hurled McMurphy across the room into the far wall.

"How many girls are we talking about?"

McMurphy staggered to his feet. "I don't know."

Maybe McMurphy didn't know, or maybe he didn't want to think about it enough to get an accurate count.

"Look, I can get you evidence. Of the buyers. We can make a deal. I'll turn over everything I know to the feds. It's a whole network. You can bring the whole thing down. I've got the proof."

"What proof?"

"Paperwork. Every transaction. Every girl, every buyer."

"Show me."

McMurphy led Connor downstairs to an office. Inside, he opened a cabinet that contained a safe. He spun the dial and, after two failed attempts, got the safe open.

Connor saw the revolver first. It was on top of a small notebook. He raised the cattle prod, ready to tee-off on McMurphy's head if he went for it, but he didn't.

"Here." McMurphy handed him the notebook.

"All the transactions are in this book?"

"That's right."

"Close the door and spin that wheel. You were smart not to go for the piece. I don't want you to reconsider that decision."

McMurphy did as Connor said.

As Connor flipped through the pages, he noticed how detailed the notes were. Victims' descriptions, dates when they arrived at the ranch, dates when they left, where they were shipped, who they were sent to, and fees collected. The only thing missing was the victims' names.

"This is a lot of evidence," said Connor.

"That's what I said. Think of how valuable that would be."

McMurphy was ready to make a deal. Turn everything over and give the government information about the higher-ups. Maybe take a cushy spot in WITSEC, move somewhere else, somewhere without horses and try life over again. That wasn't going to happen. Not because Connor didn't care about bringing people to justice, he did, he just thought there was enough information in the ledger to do that without McMurphy walking away to live life on his accord, especially since he'd taken that opportunity away for so many young women.

"That gets out and I'm a dead man," said McMurphy.

"You're already a dead man. You're just buying minutes."

"The people in that ledger, they're the real criminals. I'll roll on them. Tell the feds everything they need to know to put them away. Disrupt the whole distribution pipeline."

"Seems like everything they need is right here. Having you around might just complicate matters, don't you think?"

"I can testify."

"No, you can't."

Connor tossed the ledger on the desk and re-gripped the cattle prod. McMurphy, sensing what was coming, threw out his hands to create some distance, but it didn't help. The cattle prod connected with the fingers of his outstretched hands and it buzzed and sparked. McMurphy recoiled and fell to the floor screaming. The cattle prod had some weight. It felt like a fireplace poker in Connor's hand. He lunged again and again, connecting with McMurphy's torso, neck, and head.

When Connor got tired of the screaming, he started swinging. He brought the weapon down hard on McMurphy. Harder than the .45 on the big man in the stable. Again and again, he slammed the instrument into McMurphy, each time taking a chunk out of him.

McMurphy stopped moving after the fourth blow.

He stopped breathing after the ninth.

33

ROAD RAGE

THE POLICE LIGHTS came up fast in the rearview mirror. In the darkness, Connor couldn't make out the vehicle. Burton was out, which left the two Hatsons. Pops didn't seem like the type to get into a high-speed chase, so that left the sergeant.

Connor hit the gas and surged forward, but it didn't take long before the lights were on his bumper. He checked the mirror and saw the unmistakable chrome grill of Hatson's monstrous F-450 pickup. Hatson pulled into the left lane and moved alongside of Connor.

Connor turned and saw a shotgun staring back at him. He hit the brakes just as Hatson fired. Most of the blast missed, but the driver's door caught some buckshot. The wheels were spared.

Hatson slowed and Connor rolled down the window, slipped the .45 out, and squeezed off three rounds. He had to fire left-handed, and while he was aiming at his rear tires, all three of his shots missed.

"Where?"

The voice was coming from the back seat.

Ellie was waking up.

"Ellie? I'm a friend of your aunt Zoe's. I'm taking you to the hospital. Sit tight. And hang on."

Hatson's brake lights flashed and Connor slowed. He wanted to keep Hatson in front of him. He watched as the F-450 veered left off the road and hugged the shoulder.

He likely wanted to get out of Connor's sight line to avoid another barrage of gunfire. Or maybe he wanted Connor to pass him and make a run for it. No chance. Blow past him, and Hatson would be on his tail in a heartbeat. Connor knew he'd never outrun him. Hatson was likely running a turbocharged engine, and on a straightaway, they wouldn't stand a chance. Plus, from behind Hatson could easily ram them off the road. At high speed, all it would take would be a nudge to send Connor and Ellie into a ditch.

Why the shoulder? Another half mile and he found out.

Connor's truck barreled over a spike strip. He didn't see it until it was too late. Hatson must have laid it in advance, but he didn't know the exact location, so he took the shoulder where he knew he was safe. Connor figured he had maybe a mile left before his tires were flat. Spike strips are designed to cause slow leaks in tires, not to blow them out. Sometime soon, they'd be sitting ducks.

Ellie sat up in the back seat. "What's happening? Who are you?"

"Connor. Your red-haired friend is safe at the hospital. That's where we're headed."

"Regan?"

"If you say so. Never got her name. You're going to want to stay down."

. . .

Connor watched the rearview as Hatson dropped back. All Connor could do now was gun it. As he buried the accelerator, the truck began to rattle under the falling tire pressure. A moment later, Hatson slammed into the back of Connor's truck, knocking the .45 out of his hand and sending them careening forward. He fought to keep control as he felt Ellie crash into the back of his seat.

Hatson must have realized all he had to do was wait because he backed off. Connor's truck continued to rattle violently. As the pressure dropped further, it took everything he had to keep the truck on the road. He reached down, searching the floorboard for the .45. A piece of rubber peeled from a rim and shot into the air. He was on rims now. The metal-on-asphalt screeched like nails on a chalkboard.

The truck finally shuddered to a stop and Connor scoured the floorboard in the darkness for the weapon. He heard brakes behind him, then the F-450's door. And then the clacking of Hatson's boots. Hatson would have the shotgun in hand. He'd fire before Connor had a chance to get out of the vehicle.

He was still searching for the .45 when three shots rang out. Inside the truck's cab, the blasts were deafening, and Connor reached for his ears to stop the ringing.

When he turned to look out the window, he saw Hatson lying on the pavement, his face and neck covered in blood. Even if he had been wearing a standard issue bulletproof vest, it wouldn't have mattered.

"I know he's the bad guy," said Ellie, steadying herself in the back seat. "I feel dizzy."

"You must not be that dizzy, you hit the target."

She handed him the .45 and slid back down to the seat.

"My dad?"

"He's at the hospital. Let's go see him."

Connor pulled McMurphy's notebook from the glove box, got out of the truck, and opened the rear door for Ellie. She climbed out and stepped over Hatson.

"He doesn't look too good," said Ellie.

"Nope. But he had it coming."

Connor helped Ellie to Hatson's still idling truck. He kicked it into gear and headed for the hospital.

34

BACK TO GOOD

CONNOR HAD CALLED AHEAD, and the emergency room staff was waiting when he rolled Hatson's truck into the parking lot. Three nurses in light green scrubs scooped a semi-conscious Ellie up in a wheelchair and rolled her into the building before Connor could collect the ledger and get out of the vehicle.

When he made it to the lobby, Erin was waiting for him.

"Looks like you found her," she said.

"Things don't always work out in this business. Today they did."

"I told Aiden that you were coming. We moved him to the ER wing so he could see her."

"How's he doing?"

"He's ready to go home."

Connor nodded. "McMurphy shot Ellie up with horse tranquilizers. Suppose they did the same to Regan."

"Regan's in good shape. She's still recovering, but she's going to be just fine. Physically anyway." She led him to the elevator. "There's someone here to see you. Come on."

When Connor got off the elevator on the third floor, he was face-to-face with a black man in a navy blue suit, crisp white shirt, and no tie. The outline of a holstered sidearm was visible through his jacket.

"Who are you?" asked Connor.

"John Simmons. FBI. I hear you brought Regan Hillard in."

"Yeah. Ellie Armstrong too." He handed Simmons the notebook. "This is for you."

"What is it?"

"A ledger detailing all the women Ken McMurphy ran through the Pale Mare Ranch. Dates, dollar amounts, buyers. The women aren't identified though, just descriptions. It's a start."

Simmons flipped through the pages.

"Ginny said you were the one looking for that missing Indian girl."

"Rebecca Stillwater. She's a Shoshone."

"You ever find her?"

"No. Case went cold a long time ago. No leads."

"Well, maybe she's in that book somewhere."

"The Pale Mare Ranch, huh?"

Connor nodded.

"What am I going to find if I go out there?"

"Don't know, but McMurphy's got another house. They call it the cottage. Go there and you'll find him and two of his ranch hands, but they won't be much help to you. There's also a dead cop on the highway. Sergeant Hatson."

"Willie Hatson?"

"I guess."

"You killed a cop?"

"No."

"Start talking."

For the next hour, Connor walked Simmons through everything he knew. He chose his words carefully and made sure to leave out any incriminating information, but he knew Simmons needed details.

He told him about Tim Waters's truck, the accident, and how he figured Tim snatched Ellie from Aiden's vehicle. He told him about how he thought the accident and the abduction might be tied to something Aiden was working on, so he went to the Big Rock Police for help but the Hatsons dismissed him. He told him about the box truck and seeing Hatson at McMurphy's ranch. He explained how he found Officer Burton and Ginny at the Frontier Inn, that he figured Hatson was responsible for their murders, and that he'd find Tim Waters at the abandoned Rentschler Park mine. Finally, he recounted how he found Ellie at McMurphy's stable.

"That leaves Chief Hatson," said Simmons. "You want to tell me where I can find *him*?"

"No idea."

Simmons let out a long sigh and looked Connor up and down. "Did you leave anyone alive to corroborate any of this?"

"You might want to talk to the guy in room twenty-three. I hear he was on the wrong end of a beating. He was alive when I left him, but I wouldn't wait too long."

"Twenty-three, huh? What's his role in this?"

"Worked for McMurphy. Apparently he found himself between those two girls and their freedom."

"What's *your* role in all this? Why are you here?"

"Just a family friend."

Simmons shook his head. "You've left me with quite the cleanup. I hope you don't think you're just going to walk away from all this. That's not how it works."

"I know how it works. It's not the first time the FBI has been up my ass. Likely won't be the last either. You can call Valerie Cheatham. She's the Special Agent in Charge of the Manhattan field office. She's got my file."

"Why does that not surprise me? That there's a file."

Connor shrugged. "I'll cooperate with whatever you need, but I plan to go back to Boston as soon as possible." He rubbed his eyes. "It's too damn dry here."

Simmons flipped through the notebook again before sticking it under his arm. "I'll be in touch, Harding. I've got a lot of shit to wade through, and you're standing in the middle of it."

After Simmons disappeared down the hall, Connor ducked into an open room and sat on the bed. The hospital was eerily quiet. He glanced at the clock ticking away on the wall. It was just past one in the morning. He lay on his back and stared at the white tile ceiling, figuring it would be some time before he could talk with Ellie.

Connor liked hospitals. Most people hated them, but for some reason, he didn't mind them. He figured it was the feeling of safety. There was always someone nearby who was trained to save your life. Whether they did or not was another story, but if you needed help, this was likely the place to find it. His dry eyes were getting to him, and he closed them tight to ease the stinging. He was asleep seconds later.

·　·　·

Connor opened his eyes to Erin shaking his leg.

"Your insurance going to pay for that bed?"

He sat up and looked at the clock. He'd been asleep for six hours. "Don't you ever go home?"

"I was supposed to be off today, but I picked up an extra shift. I wanted to see how this whole thing shakes out. Plus, I have good news for you. Ellie is awake and doing well. Come on."

Connor peeled himself off the crisp white sheets and followed Erin down the same corridor they'd taken to visit Regan, but this time they went to the second floor. As she led him down the hall, he fought the urge to revisit the man in room twenty-three. He thought about it, but thought he might run into Simmons again.

At the end of the hall, in a double room that overlooked a lush courtyard, Connor found Ellie and Regan propped up in bed eating something that passed for scrambled eggs.

"Look at you two, alive and kicking," he said.

"Thanks to you," said Ellie.

"I'm just the deliveryman. From what Regan told me, you escaped on your own."

"Sure did," said Ellie. "All that and we still ended up right back where we started."

"You must be pretty tough to have gotten out and survived as long as you did. Most people in that situation wouldn't know the first thing to do. You kept your head about you. You're smart, resourceful. Kind of like your aunt. Never lose that."

"If it wasn't for Ellie," said Regan, "I don't know where I'd be right now. She's a Goddamned beast. I just wish Jen would have gotten out with us."

"Who's that?"

"She was in the basement with us, but they took her somewhere else. Just before we broke out."

"I picked up a ledger at McMurphy's house. It had a list of the women he's moved in and out of the ranch. The FBI has it now, and I'm sure they'll be on it. Maybe they can find Jen."

"If she can stay alive that long," said Regan.

"People are usually tougher than they give themselves credit for," said Connor. "I have a good feeling about Special Agent Simmons. He seems like the kind of person who gets shit done."

"Like you?" said Aiden from a chair in the corner.

"Yeah, like me."

"About my aunt, why did she send you?"

"The hospital called her after your father ended up in the ER. Found her phone number in his wallet. She called your cell phone and got worried when she couldn't find you."

"What I meant was, why did she send *you*?"

"Because I was the best man for the job."

Ellie set her plate on the rollaway table next to the bed. "I can't argue with that."

"You three take care. Sorry we had to meet under these circumstances. I hope you're all back to good soon."

Connor turned and headed for the hallway. He decided not tell them that the man they almost killed was on the same floor. He thought they might go finish the job.

"When you see my aunt, will you tell her to call me?" Ellie tapped the beige phone on the table. "Just tell her what room we're in."

"Don't worry. I'd bet she already knows. That's kind of her thing."

Connor had one foot in the hall when the phone rang.

35

ALL SQUARE

Two days later, Connor arrived at his home in Boston. Special Agent Simmons had everything he needed to start an investigation into McMurphy's activities. At the speed the government worked that might take years, but at least it was moving forward.

Erin had told him she expected Aiden and Ellie would be out of the hospital in a matter of days. Aiden would be looking at extensive physical therapy, but at least he could go home. She also told Connor she overheard Regan saying something about moving to Wyoming. Not Big Rock, but maybe Cheyenne or Casper.

Connor moved to the kitchen and opened a bottle of root beer. When he returned to the living room, he found Zoe standing in his doorway.

"Ever hear of a telephone?" said Connor.

"I figured this warranted an in-person visit."

"The last time you said that, I ended up on an airplane to Wyoming. I'm not planning any more trips."

"I wouldn't ask. I meant that what you did out there

warranted an in-person thank you. You dismantled a human trafficking operation. That's got to make you feel good."

"I guess." Connor watched his reflection in Zoe's mirrored sunglasses. "But I do have one question."

"What's that?"

"What were you moving through Wyoming?"

"What are you talking about?"

"I figured McMurphy snatched Ellie for revenge and assumed, like you suggested, that it was likely tied to Aiden's work with the feds."

"Right."

"But I talked to Aiden, and he's a researcher. He's not even directly on the payroll. He's a consultant."

"And?"

"And I don't see the connection. Can't see the motive for McMurphy going after Aiden and his daughter if Aiden isn't even an agent."

Zoe crossed her arms. "What are you saying?"

"I'm saying that I don't think McMurphy even knew Aiden worked with the FBI. But then I got to thinking about McMurphy's distribution network. He was running horses across the country. Those distribution channels are what generated the trafficking business. It's how he moved girls around from one place to another. And then I thought, if he was moving people, he was likely moving other things for people like you. So, what were you moving through Wyoming, Zoe?"

"I knew I sent you for a reason."

Connor didn't respond.

"It was heroin, and it was years ago. I was going through Wyoming and Montana into Canada. The DEA busted it up and a lot of people went down. I was able to keep my name out of it."

"And McMurphy was your local contact?"

"Yeah. He lost a lot of people and blamed me. He thought the feds were onto me and that I somehow led them to Casper."

"Were they investigating you?"

"The feds have been investigating me for decades, Connor. Got my own task force and everything. But I didn't slip up and lead them to Casper. They must have already been working that angle."

"And you didn't think to tell me that the man you screwed over may have had something to do with Ellie's disappearance?"

"I had no idea he was trafficking women. If I had known that, I would have put a stop to it a long time ago."

"You know everything, Zoe. That's kind of your business."

"Fuck you, Connor. I wouldn't have worked with him. And I had no idea he was behind Ellie's disappearance, or I would have sent you straight to his doorstep. The Casper bust was forever ago. No reason to believe he was connected to any of this."

Connor sat on his couch and propped his feet up on the coffee table.

"I would have never done anything to risk the safety of my family, Connor. You know me better than that."

Connor stared at his reflection in Zoe's sunglasses again, wishing he could get a glimpse of her eyes. "That's good enough for me."

"Well, thank you," she said. "For everything you did."

"You're welcome."

She turned and went for the door.

"We square, Zoe? Because we really need to be."

She didn't turn around. "We're square. See you around."

Connor watched her walk out his front door. He lifted the root beer bottle to his lips. It was the coldest thing he'd tasted in days.

WILL CONNOR HARDING RETURN?

Will Connor Harding return? Maybe, but why not check out the Finn Harding series while the author makes up his mind? We suggest starting with:

The Shadow Broker

A private investigator must unravel a blackmail plot targeting a criminal information brokerage before the FBI and a hired killer stop him.

Finn Harding specializes in finding people who don't want to be found. Bishop runs a black-market information brokerage on the dark web, selling stolen personal data to the highest bidder.

When someone blackmails Bishop, threatening to go public with his identity and crimes, he hires Finn to find the person behind the plot. During his investigation, Finn draws the attention of the FBI's cybercrime unit investigating Bishop, a psychopathic hitman hired to take out the blackmailer, and a Detroit mob boss hellbent on taking over Bishop's operation.

As Finn gets closer to unraveling the mystery, he discovers

his ex-wife and young daughter have become targets in the sinister conspiracy.

Can Finn survive long enough to unmask the blackmailer, save his family, and escape the FBI's and the mob's grasp?

The Shadow Broker novel won a Shamus Award from the P.I. Writers of America as one of the best crime books of the year.

AUTHOR'S NOTE

If you want to stay on top of my new releases, get free fiction, or snag exclusive deals, sign up for my author newsletter at www.traceconger.com/freebies.

If you liked this book, consider leaving a review at your favorite online bookstore. Reviews from readers like you can help other readers find their next favorite read. And it's a great way to support your favorite authors.

Thanks for the eyeballs.

Trace Conger
Cincinnati, Ohio

ACKNOWLEDGMENTS

I have many goals as an author. One is to surround myself with encouraging people who not only support me but also make me a better writer. I want to thank the following people for their involvement in bringing this story to life.

Andrew Bockhold for reading early drafts and helping me guide this story through the rapids. Jeff Hillard for reviewing not-so-early drafts and helping me pull this boat ashore. Elizabeth White for taking a heap of words and making it look like a prettier heap of words. April Wilson and the Miami Valley Writers Network for sharing your battle scars and knowledge.

Thank you also to the Crossed Sabres Ranch in Wyoming for the must-see-to-believe views and for convincing me not to set this novel in Kentucky.

And finally, thank you to my amazing family, who encourage and inspire me every day.

ABOUT THE AUTHOR

Trace Conger is an award-winning author in the crime, thriller, and suspense genres. He writes the Connor Harding (Thriller) series and the Mr. Finn (PI) series, among others.

His Connor Harding series follows freelance "Mirage Man" Connor Harding as he solves problems for the world's most dangerous criminals. The Mr. Finn series follows private investigator Finn Harding as he straddles the fine line between right and wrong.

Conger won a Shamus Award for his debut novel, THE SHADOW BROKER. His suspense novella, THE WHITE BOY, won the Fresh Ink Award for Best Novella of 2020.

He is known for his tight writing style, dark themes, and subtle humor. Trace lives in Cincinnati with his wonderfully supportive family.

ALSO BY TRACE CONGER

<u>Mr. Finn Series:</u>

The Shadow Broker

Scar Tissue

The Prison Guard's Son

<u>Connor Harding Series:</u>

Catch and Release

Mirage Man

The Wicked Side

<u>Standalones:</u>

The White Boy

Five Will Die